Men into space

Murray Leinster

1

(When Ed McCauley was a very young officer—in fact, a new-made first lieutenant, space travel was restricted to robots. They did good work, for robots, but it wasn't enough. No man had ever gone up in a rocket. Nobody had ever gone up—let alone land safely. So the time came when somebody had to. And in those very early days McCauley volunteered for the job and managed to get it.)

***

First Lieutenant Ed McCauley opened his eyes and looked at the ceiling, wondering drowsily why this morning seemed so much more satisfying and important than any other. He'd had a good sleep, even though he remembered vaguely that he'd had a hard time dropping off. Now the sunlight came through the window blind in slatted streaks, the wall was a pale tan, and he was lying on an iron cot, his uniform neatly draped over a chair. Then he heard voices and the clattering of china, and suddenly he remembered where he was and what was important about today.

Today was the day of the shoot. The rocket shoot. It wasn't going to be big and spectacular, with a multiple-stage giant looming so high that a man couldn't see the payload capsule on top without his neck creaking. There'd be no giant gantry crane hovering over a slim but monstrous missile with its hundreds of plugged-in wires recording the performances of some tens of thousands of separate parts, all of which had to work perfectly if one part were to be any good. Even the electric wires had to pull clear perfectly when the gantry crane rolled back a matter of seconds before the end of the count down.

No. This shoot wouldn't be spectacular. There weren't even any reporters around. Official Service cameramen would record what happened; and if all went well there'd be plenty of excitement about it later, and if all didn't go well it wouldn't matter too much.

This time there was no publicity buildup. Nobody'd be disappointed if things went wrong. The only person who'd feel badly was First Lieutenant Ed McCauley, and he wouldn't feel it too keenly. In fact, he wouldn't feel anything.

He'd be dead.

He considered the idea for a moment, but when a person is First Lieutenant McCauley's age, dying is something that happens to somebody else. You can't imagine it happening to you. It's a sort of reverse of being born, but you can't imagine that either, though it happened.

He sat up and kicked his feet over the side of the cot. He felt a little bit relieved. He was excited, now that he remembered what was in the works for today, but it wasn't a solemn feeling. He got up and looked at himself in the small square mirror over the washstand. He looked exactly as he always did. He felt the same way. Well-l, maybe a little more awake and alive than usual, because he'd been horribly afraid that something would happen and the shoot would be called off. But it hadn't—so far.

He went down the hall to the showers, trailing a towel over his shoulder. He showered, thinking zestfully about the prospects. There'd be no trouble about the weather. At this base clouds were exceptional and a cloud cover that hindered even visual tracking was almost unknown. Suddenly he wanted to sing, but he restrained himself. As lucky as he felt, it might sound like showing off.

The door of the shower room opened and somebody came in.

"Hi, National Hero. You in there?" It was Randy's voice, slightly sardonic.

"Ain't nobody here but us chickens, boss," McCauley answered cheerfully. "Nary a hero."

Randy grunted.

"How d'you feel, Ed?"

"Wet," said McCauley. He turned off the shower and began to towel himself. When he emerged, Randy searched his face, his anxiety showing on his own.

"Nope," said McCauley, "the condemned man's got a good appetite for breakfast. Quit worrying about me, Randy!"

"If you'd only slipped on your soap and broken your doggone neck," Randy complained, "a good guy might've gotten a chance to take your place!"

McCauley grinned. Randy would give his eyeteeth to take his place today. Anybody would. McCauley still worried that even now something would spoil things, but he'd been worrying for months. He'd been jumpy ever since the rumor first went around that sometime soon somebody was going up in a rocket and coming down again. Nobody ever had. Up to this morning it was still waiting to be done. But somebody—in fact, he himself—should do it today. This was why today was the most special day of his life.

Back in his quarters he shaved, marveling at the luck of the man he saw in the mirror. Three—four—five months ago he'd been telling himself that he didn't have a chance of being picked, even though he was sure he'd put in for it as soon as anybody had. He'd hoped he'd been the first to apply, but actually he was one of two hundred. They'd winnowed the applicants, though, and four months ago twenty were left, and then only ten. Now there was only himself in first place, with four other bitterly envious characters—Randy was one of them—wishing he'd break his neck so they could go in his place.

But nothing like that would happen if he could help it. Washing the shaving soap off his face, he found himself praying that everything would go all right. He didn't think of asking that he come down safely; after all, he could insure his safety by backing out. He just asked that he'd be all right when they checked him over, and that the count down would go all right, and that he'd get up to where the sky turned purple and then black and he saw the stars shining bright, with the sun among them as the nearest and greatest star of all. And he prayed that he'd do the right things while he was up there so the shoot would be a success.

He settled his uniform and went to breakfast. Randy had ordered for him and was waiting. Randy still looked worried. He'd tried hard for the job for himself, but now he was afraid that his friend McCauley might not check out. That the rocket might not check out. That when he got up there something might go wrong. That coming down would be bad.

"Soft-boiled," said McCauley appreciatively, breaking an egg. "My favorite fruit!"

"Do you really feel okay, Ed?" asked Randy.

McCauley grinned again, which was answer enough. Maybe he felt too good. He probably should tone down a little. After all, this shoot with a man as the payload wasn't a pleasure trip. It was research. It was an operation to verify other research. The medicos believed they knew what the psychological, physiological, and emotional effects of long-continued weightlessness would be. They needed to know how a normal man like McCauley would react to the unparalleled environment of nearer space. It was high-altitude research, primarily to enable planes to fly faster. A plane could be powered right now so that its wings would melt at sea level because of the heat its speed produced. The only way to reach theoretical top speed in a plane was to fly it away up. There was a thermal barrier to really high-speed flight. The only way around this barrier was over it, and it was necessary to find out how a man would make out in that detour. The Service had a long-established custom of spending a dollar instead of a man; now it had not to spend a man perhaps, but to risk one. And McCauley was the man.

He felt remarkably good, knowing that presently he should be where no man had ever been before, seeing with his own eyes that the earth was round. It struck him suddenly that everybody else in the world had only indirect evidence for believing this. He'd be the first man to know this for a fact simply because he'd gone up to where he would see the earth as a ball.

"No shivers?" asked Randy presently, as if in envy. "Wouldn't you rather not and say you did? I'll take over for you!"

"Don't tempt me!" said McCauley, pushing his cup across the table. "And how about some more coffee?"

Randy grunted. Maybe he'd been ordered to do some kidding, so McCauley wouldn't get the wind up. But it didn't matter to Ed. If only everything went all right at the blockhouse everything would have to go all right all along the line. But the chance that things might be fouled up there made him want to keep his fingers crossed. Yes. The blockhouse was the big hurdle. Anything that happened after that wouldn't be failure on his part. He wanted to pray again, this time about the blockhouse. But he didn't.

The two men left the officers'-quarters building together. There was a jeep waiting, with Sergeant Hall at its wheel.

"Mornin', Lieuten't. How you feeling?"

The sergeant looked at McCauley with the same combination of envy and anxiety that Randy had shown—envy for what McCauley had ahead of him, anxiety for whether he felt all right so that he could go through with it.

"Look!" said McCauley, annoyed. "I'm all right! There's nothing to worry about! The thing's been done before with instruments, dummies, monkeys, and now it's me. I'm just another ape. That's all! For the love of Saint Aloysius stop worrying!"

Sergeant Hall let in the clutch.

"Okay, Lieuten't," he said mildly. "I was just going to wish you good luck."

"Cross your fingers against the medics," said McCauley dourly. "I never liked doctors. I've got to get by some of them."

He settled back in the jeep and it went bolting out into the already blazing sunlight beyond the shadow of the building.

The landscape wasn't pretty—sun-baked clay and sand on the road, and mesquite and more mesquite all around. The sunshine was hotter here than anywhere else in the world. It was still long before noon, but already the horizon shimmered in the heat and occasional little sand-devils rose up half-heartedly and then subsided as if it were too hot even for whirlwinds. Far away there were the mountains. McCauley had gone over there once, and they'd towered impossibly toward the sky. But presently he'd have trouble picking them out because they'd be so small and the ground so nearly flat. Heat beat up from the ground and through the windshield. After a quarter of an hour he could see the spindly launching tower—no gantry cranes here!—above one of the ridges over which the jeep went rolling, kicking up a monstrous cloud of yellow dust behind it.

McCauley didn't mind the heat. He felt remarkably aware of being alive and breathing, of the sunlight, and of a wrinkle in his pants on the jeep seat. After a little he saw the flat roof of the blockhouse. Then he felt scared. He was afraid of the blockhouse. There'd be a last checkup to make sure he was perfectly all right, perfectly normal, no more tense than the doctors decided was allowable, and so on. His heart began to pound a little and he agonized over it. If they decided it was acting queer....

He found himself praying again. Please, God, don't let them find anything wrong with me! I want so much to do this!

Randy didn't look at him. A good guy, Randy. He'd know it was panic over those doggone doctors poking stethoscopes at him and going off to mutter together about what they'd heard.

"Randy, if I look scared, it's because I am," McCauley said between his teeth. "There's a medic in that blockhouse who wanted his brother-in-law to get this job. He'd be just the kind to mess me up now!"

Randy offered a cigarette. McCauley shook his head.

The blockhouse was sunk in the dry earth. It was concrete, yards thick, with nothing visible from this side except a deep-sunk door in the wall. On the other side there was a narrow slit to look out of, and there were periscopes and in a pit over yonder the close-by trackers. There were other trackers in other spots—as far away as the mountains. But there wasn't much of anything to be seen here.

... No. There was the rocket. One of the new big Aerobees. Nothing fancy about it. The Atlas and the long-distance jobs generally got all the publicity these days. But the Aerobees were solid and workmanlike, veteran performers. Fancy hardware broke the records and was what people meant when they talked about missiles and rockets, but Aerobees were the workhorses that went up without fanfare, got the information they were sent up for, and got it back down again. It was an Aerobee that had proved matter-of-factly that most of the stuff in the textbooks about the upper air simply wasn't so. Aerobees were the first to disprove the belief that the tropopause was a motionless, featureless calm belt up aloft. Aerobees brought back conclusive evidence of vertical currents in that supposed utter calm, currents that shot upward at three hundred meters per second. And it was Aerobees that brought back proof of ultraviolet light reaching Earth on its dark side, so the theory boys could go quietly mad figuring out where the light came from.

Yes. The pointed nose and sleek shape of the Aerobee was a comfort, standing by its straight-up launching tower. McCauley'd seen dozens of shoots of Aerobees. He felt the affection a man feels for something that does its job competently and casually, day in and day out, when called upon to do it.

The jeep stopped. Randy got out and McCauley followed him. The sergeant opened his mouth but thought better of it. He drove away without saying anything more about luck.

The doorway of the blockhouse was cool. Inside, as the door closed behind him, McCauley felt the air-conditioned chill and the clatter of the place almost as if he'd been struck a blow. There were people everywhere. Practically everybody wore a phone headset and chest microphone and everybody was talking to somebody somewhere else, paying no attention to anyone nearby.

McCauley stood still, waiting to be told where to go. Somebody called to him:

"The docs aren't ready for you yet, Lieutenant. You're early."

"Okay," McCauley said. "Where'll I go to get out of the way?"

It didn't look as if anybody else could possibly wait around in the blockhouse without further fouling up the already-present confusion.

"Let's go look at the transportation," Randy suggested.

McCauley shrugged and followed Randy outside. It was comforting that nobody paid any attention to him. At least the people in charge of the shoot weren't worrying about his not being okayed for the job.

In the sunshine again, he saw familiar things. The close-by trackers in their pits, sunk below ground level in case something blew. The telemeter receivers looked like huge wire bowls, decorated with rolls of toilet tissue, aimed at the sky. They moved back and forth, testing. They'd get back telemetered information and sort it out and make tapes of it, and whoever read those tapes would know more about what was happening than McCauley did. A telemetering system will sample a practically indefinite number of instrument readings three hundred times a second and send back the information in wild banshee howls or else in scratchy noises that sound like all the static in the world coming out of one loudspeaker.

Even so, things were better than they used to be, for there was a time when not nearly so much information got back. For that matter, McCauley'd heard about the tame German scientist—formerly of Peenemünde—who used to stand out in the open behind the blockhouse when those first rockets went up, sweating and squinting and saying, "Goot!" "Goot!" as long as he could see that things were going well, and sputtering despairingly and unintelligibly in German when they went wrong.

They went wrong pretty often in the beginning, back ten years or so ago. There was the time a rocket went up and simply vanished. All the trackers lost it and nobody had the least idea where it'd gone. All the men sat around biting their nails and wondering where in blazes it was. Finally there'd been a telephone call from a woman in Alamogordo. She'd managed to reach someone with authority to route her call though to the blockhouse.

"Ah hear you folks are shootin' up rockets," she said in an indignant drawl. "Well, you-all better come an' get your rocket outa my backyard right now!"

It had landed in her backyard, many miles away, and it had missed her house by no more than twenty feet.

Another time—a long, long while ago—a V-2 tied itself into knots and headed for Mexico. When it came down near Juarez, all the Mexicans for miles around came on the run with hacksaws. After they'd cut off pieces of it for "space souvenirs," there wasn't much left to be hauled back to base....

McCauley followed Randy around to the front. They walked over the hot sandy ground to the launching tower. There was a fuel truck there, and the sickly-sweet but bitter smell of hydrazine. The fueling gang wore plastic coveralls with hoods and clear plastic faceplates. McCauley knew this process; he'd helped with it. But today he kept carefully out of the way. The fueling gang was finicky about its work. Each man was extravagantly careful not to spill a drop of hydrazine, because if somebody stepped on a drop that had spilled and then, later on, stepped on a drop of nitric that had spilled, he'd have a hotfoot to end all hotfoots—on that foot, anyhow, because he wouldn't have it any longer.

The hydrazine topped off. The truck went away, with everything carefully closed up lest a drop of anything spill on to the ground. The fueling gang went to change coveralls, for they wore coveralls of a different color when they were going to load up the nitric acid. Never the twain—hydrazine and nitric—should meet until pumped together into a rocket engine.

The Aerobee was tall and sleek and smooth and streamlined, but now there were ladders leaning against it. Somebody was working through a door in the sidewall. McCauley went around and glanced at the guide rail. The Aerobee used a short-time booster to start up. The booster ran up the rail to the top of the launching tower and then landed somewhere nearby. But the Aerobee would keep on going. By the time it reached the top of the tower and the end of the guide rail, it should be going fast enough for its fins to have some grip on the air. When the air got too thin to be of any use, the steam-jets working from the fin tips should guide it.

The nitric acid truck came slowly into position. It didn't cross the track the hydrazine truck had taken, and stopped in an entirely different place; the fueling crew reappeared, in their different-colored plastic coveralls. The precautions taken against the premature introduction of hydrazine and nitric acid were remarkable.

McCauley let himself look up once at the nose-cone. He'd tried it on for size before. In it, he was going to have to take the launching jolt of more gees than any jet pilot has to be prepared for. But he felt a serene confidence that he could do it.

Then somebody called:

"Hey! Lieutenant! They want you back at the blockhouse!"

McCauley turned back obediently. The fuel gang was pumping in the nitric as he left. It stank, and he knew that if the smell gets under the faceplate of your hood you throw back the hood and faceplate together and gasp for breath. He realized that he wasn't breathing too easily. The doctors were going to make their final check on him, and what they said would be it. He felt the familiar panicky conviction that they'd find something wrong with him. For instance, panic would be something wrong.

He caught hold of himself as he and Randy entered the blockhouse. Somehow the confusion and busyness of everybody there were reassuring. On the way to where the doctors waited, he heard people talking into telephones about wind velocities and barometric pressures and how in thunder did that civilian automobile get into the test area? Somebody had to get it out fast, because there was a shoot on, in case nobody'd heard. The last was pure sarcasm.

Anyhow the technical crew thought he was all right. So McCauley submitted himself to the doctors in a sort of truculent readiness to put up an argument if they said anything critical of his condition or his readiness to go where nobody had ever gone before. With everything else all ready, they'd have a nerve to suggest anything but a go-ahead!

They took his blood pressure and did a cardiogram, and they put a tape around his chest and a stylus drew a crazy curve which showed the way he was breathing. Then they took samples of his breath and his blood and other body fluids, and his temperature and the electrical resistance of his skin and forty-seven other things. They'd done all this before. They'd done it while he was resting and while he was taking hard exercise, when he was tired and when he'd just waked up from a good night's sleep.

They had blown-up pictures of every square inch of his skin, so they could check for sputters at high altitude. A sputter might occur if a cosmic particle at just the right speed happened to hit him. He hadn't any privacy left. The docs knew everything about him, except that he was absolutely the right person for man's first ascent in a pure rocket, and his return to Earth in one piece. No rocket had ever landed intact, of course. They smashed. Invariably. But a way had been worked out to get instruments back unshattered. That was the way he'd land.

One of the doctors nodded.

"With that pulse rate your system's pumping out plenty of adrenalin. That's good!"

McCauley relaxed a little. He watched as they checked his reflexes. He could tell that they looked all right, anyway. They gave him a pencil and timed him while he did a page of IQ stuff. In the past few weeks they'd established his personal norm for all sorts of things, and now they were checking to see whether anticipation pushed him too far off normal. He began to sweat when he realized that he needed to act exactly as usual, and they knew it, and he sweated more because of it. They checked him over as they would a guinea pig before an experiment, only he was the guinea pig. But he was desperately anxious for all this to be over and for the experiment to start.

Presently they finished and looked at each other and nodded. Then one of them said, "You'll do," and McCauley went almost sick with relief. Then, infuriatingly, he knew from their expressions that they'd looked for exactly that reaction. He couldn't do anything they wouldn't analyze and think about. And he burned a little, but it was all right. Everything was all right!

When Ed came out to the main part of the blockhouse again, Randy knew from his expression that he'd been checked out for the flight, but he asked politely:

"Mother and child doing well?"

By that time McCauley wanted to hug somebody for sheer joy, but instead he said sedately,

"The doc says I'm a boy."

But just the same he was almost weak from the reaction to the ending of his fears about what the doctors might decide. He looked at his watch. Just about on schedule. Over in a corner somebody with a headphone and chest mike was marking off items on a list he had before him. He said, "Telemeter circuits," and paused. A voice evidently sounded in his headphones, because he made a checkmark with his pencil. Then he said, "Tracker circuits," and waited, and made another checkmark. As McCauley walked on to where his voice was drowned out, he was still saying toneless things into his chest mike and making checkmarks after unhearable replies.

Randy closed the door of the cubicle where McCauley would

11

put on the grav-suit. It was skin-tight and festooned all over with stray bits of equipment. Randy helped him get into it.

"Lucky son-of-a-gun!" he said conversationally. "How do the Irish get all the breaks?"

"Clean living," McCauley told him, "and a drag with the top brass."

It wasn't so, of course. Not the top brass part, anyhow.

His arm caught in the right sleeve and Randy helped him straighten it. There were peculiar tubes built into the fabric. They were all hooked to a grav-valve that would let compressed air into them at a suitable pressure to tighten the suit and fight the tendency of his blood and inner organs to be left behind when his bones and flesh were accelerated by the full thrust of the rocket. A man wasn't built to stand the acceleration he had to take. But the grav-suit would make up the difference.

He turned slowly around, and Randy inspected everything with the jealous care of somebody who'll never forgive himself if anything goes wrong. Presently he said:

"Flip it—but be careful!"

McCauley touched the test-stud. The tubes expanded. The suit tightened. It felt as if it were going to try to squeeze his whole body out through the neck. He lifted his hand and the squeezing stopped. Randy screwed up the test-stud so it couldn't flip on by accident. He felt of the chute-pack that was part of the suit, with the wide straps that went around McCauley's body and thighs. He checked the four trailing cables—each with a different-shaped plug on its end—that would pass along all the suit-instrumentation news to the telemeter transmitter.

Then Randy nodded worriedly and gave McCauley a cigarette.

"It looks okay," he said. But he fretted.

"Everything's okay," said McCauley.

He puffed contentedly. When the cigarette was half-smoked, somebody tapped on the door.

"You can get aboard, Lieutenant."

McCauley stood up. Randy opened the door for him and he went ambling clumsily through the blockhouse toward the exit. He heard a toneless voice say: "Crash wagon two"; then the man listened and made a checkmark. Somebody else snapped: "Tell the idiot that we're trying to keep him out of range of a few tons of hardware that'll be coming down out of the sky presently. Sit on his head!" That would be the official response to the civilian motorist's objection to being kept safely off the test site when a shoot was on.

McCauley went on out into the open air. He felt weighty and clumsy and cumbersome. He went around the blockhouse and into the blazing sunshine. The fueling crew was finished, but they hadn't left. They waited to watch him go aboard. There was a ladder leaning against the Aerobee. McCauley plodded heavily to the foot of it. He put his foot on the first rung and turned to Randy.

"Here I go."

"Yeah," said Randy. He didn't smile. He couldn't. But he did have a fine air of nonchalance as he said, "See you soon."

There was no handshake. It would have been too much like saying good-by. McCauley started up the ladder.

It was a long climb; and three-quarters of the way up, with all the assorted gimmicks and the clumsy chute-pack banging against his buttocks, he began to breathe fast. Once he stepped on a trailing cable. He looked down and was annoyed to find that the height bothered him—a man who would presently be up many miles higher than any man had ever been before. And this was only tens of feet, yet he felt giddy! He didn't look down again.

He reached the door in the nose-cone and climbed in. He'd practiced it. He felt easier when he was inside. Up here, on top of several tons of rocket fuel, he felt safer because there was a floor under him. He grimaced at the foolishness of it. Rocket fuel is highly explosive; a rocket works because a continuous explosion is taking place in its engine. But McCauley felt safer sitting on enough hydrazine and nitric to blow him to atoms than coming up a narrow, springy ladder.

Laboriously he settled himself. The acceleration chair had been tailored to fit him in this suit. He got the trailing cables clear and made himself comfortable. Then he waited. He could stir a little, but not much. It was, of course, extremely comforting to be able to move his feet in even limited swings.

The nose-cone door darkened. Somebody reached in and

plugged the cables into their proper sockets. He hauled straps from nowhere and buckled them.

"Here's your helmet, Lieutenant," he said.

"Thanks," said McCauley.

He put it on. Air began to flow past his face and he knew that all the gadgets in his suit were hooked in, and that back in the blockhouse they could count his breaths and tell how deep they were, they were getting a continuous cardiogram to tell how his heart was working, and they had a running record of his blood pressure. If he panicked now they'd know it. The man outside the nose-cone door poked around like a hen fussing over a solitary chick. McCauley wished he'd go away. A voice sounded in the helmet earphones.

"Checking phones. Do you hear me?"

"Sure," said McCauley. "I hear all right."

The phones clicked and were silent. The nose-cone door closed and McCauley was alone. Somehow he felt naked, because he knew that everything he felt and almost everything he thought was going on record via telemeter in the blockhouse. It was dark here.... No, two small electric bulbs were glowing. One was a spare. He saw the stuff laid out for later.

He knew what went on outside, but it was what was going on inside him that disturbed him. He didn't want the instruments in his suit to report anything wrong. He wanted to do this job right! For that reason he was consciously patient while he knew that men clinging to the launching tower were pulling away the last-minute cords that had been reporting everything functioning just right. Then everybody'd be getting out of the way. The Aerobee stood silent and still above a concrete pit filled with water. Somebody would use a last few seconds to coil up a cable that should have been put away before. In seconds now, though, everyone would pop out of sight. Over by the mountains they'd be working the trackers there to make sure they were all right. There'd be the warning blast. It ought to be about now. Ten—nine—eight—

A voice came into the helmet phones.

"Forty seconds more, Lieutenant. Everything's going fine so far!"

McCauley had a momentary impulse to try to make some crack or other that would be appropriate, express how he felt, and so on. But he didn't feel as he'd expected to. And anything like that would sound like showing off. So he just answered matter-of-factly:

"That's good."

He waited. And waited. And waited. And waited.

The voice in his helmet phones said abruptly:

"Ten seconds ... Nine ... Eight ... Seven ... Six ... Five ... Four ... Three ... Two ... One...."

During the last second McCauley remembered to put his arms in the armrests, because the acceleration was going to be all he could take. All. If his arms hung down, the blood would engorge his fingers and swell them to uselessness. He was already scrounged down in place, and he had his chin in the chinrest of the helmet—the whole helmet had a fitting to support it—so if he blacked out his tongue wouldn't slide back down his throat and strangle him.

Something hit him. It hit him all over at the same instant, as if he were being slammed in a million places by a million six-ounce gloves all at once. Something grabbed his legs and squeezed his belly and blew air in his face, and the roar was numbing, but he didn't remember hearing it begin. He'd expected all of it but he reacted by quite automatically getting raging mad. He knew he was on the way up and he felt thrilled and furious and he hurt all over, simultaneously.

It was agony, but if he could have grinned he'd have done it. Everything had gone off all right! Nothing was wrong! It was too late for anything to stop the shoot now! It was happening!

His stomach felt terrifically tight against the corset-like front of the grav-suit. The legs squeezed—hard! That puff of wind was extra air pressure to protect his lungs. He suffered, and he was half blind, and he fought for breath, but that extra air pressure helped a lot. All the blood tried to come down out of his brain and his cheeks sagged and his ears would have flopped down if it weren't for the headphones holding them flat against his head.

Suddenly things were easier. The booster'd burned out and dropped off. McCauley remembered to grunt, to say that he hadn't lost consciousness in the first intolerable getaway acceleration. The two small electric bulbs had seemed to turn reddish. He made a mental note to mention it presently. The pressure was still monstrous. He seemed to weigh tons—actually he did weigh an appreciable part of one—but his weight was less than it had been. That first slamming was the take-off, lasting barely seconds though it felt like long minutes. This second-stage acceleration would last more than a minute. It would seem like hours.

It did. McCauley's muscles were already getting weary of lifting his whole chest for breathing when a voice said in the phones: "Beautiful shoot! Beautiful! Everything's going fine!" He grunted in acknowledgment. It would be too much effort to talk. Also he felt an obscure anger, which was his body's reaction to the unreasonable suffering imposed upon it. A little green light flashed, and he was supposed to grunt at it, and he did.

He grunted a second time when it flashed again. Quickly. A third and fourth and fifth time. Something would be learned from the quickness with which he could respond to signals during this second-stage thrust. A pause, and the green light flashed and kept on flashing too fast for him to respond, and he said, "Cripes!" very wearily. Then it stopped.

The roaring went on and on, and abruptly there were violent coughings below. Instantly his head tried to split wide open because the acceleration ceased between two heartbeats, while his heart kept on trying to pump blood against a static head which was many times normal, and suddenly there was no static head at all. There was no gravity to be pumped against. There was no weight to anything. Then his heart tried to adjust to that, and it skipped beats, and all his insides that had been dragged downward now rose up and tried to climb out of his throat.

He gagged and swallowed.

"Okay!" he panted. "In free fall! The light changed to reddish but it's back to normal. I feel fighting mad. Over."

"First puzzle," said a brisk voice in the headphones.

McCauley reached out into the arrangement of objects before him. He took out a puzzle. It wasn't complicated, but he had to recognize it and then remember how to do it. He tossed it aside, finished, and his working time was undoubtedly recorded. The voice said:

"Name two things in the same class among these: robin, shovel, tree, ibis, shark."

McCauley answered. Again the time was noted. This was straight IQ stuff, to see how soon and how well his brain was functioning after the beating he'd taken in the booster-stage take-off and the second-stage acceleration of the rocket itself. He knew what it was all about, even when they told him to solve puzzle six, and then four, and then asked more silly questions. He responded as well as he could, with no idea how good that was. But he felt a great irrational anger and indignation. When he was asked to recite a paragraph of prose he'd memorized for the exact purpose of reciting it, on demand, he recited it. But he was unreasonably angry. It was his body's response to the suffering just past.

Presently he snapped:

"Doggone it, I want to see something!"

"Go ahead," said the voice from the ground. "But keep on talking. It doesn't matter what you say. Talk."

He pressed the button that slid the port shutters aside. The shutters were necessary. There'd been terrific heat outside when the nose-cone flung upward through the denser lower atmosphere near ground level. He looked eagerly out.

For a moment he couldn't speak. He saw the horizon as an almost white line against a star-specked black sky. It was curved! There were innumerable flecks of whiteness—they'd be clouds—below him; they grew thicker farther away. He saw the ocean, which was hundreds of miles away. The world visibly tilted downwards, downhill away from him. He looked below and it was paradoxically a bowl. Quite close he saw a fleeting, rushing, tormented spurt of vapor which vanished instantly. It was a steam-jet correcting yaw or spin or tumbling, up here where the air was so thin that the fins themselves could take no grip on it.

Years ago, when a WAC corporal made the first flight up to the then incredible height of two hundred and fifty miles, the machine turned end for end five times as it rose, and its tumbling made no difference. It was practically in a vacuum. McCauley was higher than that, already. But this Aerobee pointed straight, balanced by little puffings of steam. It didn't even rotate.

He could see stars all around, and then he turned to the one filtered port and looked at the sun through it. It was a monstrous brilliance, with writhing fire-fringes around its edges. He saw Mercury off to its right. It was the first time in his life that he'd ever seen that planet, and he'd had to get out of the atmosphere to do it. Not one person in ten thousand has ever seen the sun's closest satellite, even as a tiny speck of light in the sky. But McCauley saw it, not hidden by the daytime sky. There was no air here to speak of. At this height a man not in a pressure-tight cabin, trying to breathe what few molecules of air were present, would die in thirteen seconds because of anoxia and explosive decompression. He'd die no more quickly out between the galaxies.

"Keep talking," said the voice in the headphones. "Keep talking, man!"

McCauley found himself stammering. What he said wasn't particularly coherent, and he knew his taped speech would be studied to find out exactly what mental state he was in. The headphones asked questions. Could he see this? Could he see that? He answered yes and no. The voice asked him to write something. He did, not looking at it. He stared out at the monstrousness of the universe, with Earth merely a dimpled gigantic ball below him.

He had no weight, but he did not notice. He gazed and gazed and exulted, and absent-mindedly obeyed the orders which came insistently to his ears. He wanted to saturate his mind and his memory with the sight that nobody had ever seen before, except in pictures taken at this height by robots.

Presently the sky wasn't totally black with innumerable tiny lights in it. It was a deep, dark purple. The stars seemed fainter. He said so.

"Right," said the voice in his helmet. "You reached peak altitude minutes ago. You're well on the way back down, now. We're going to turn the rocket over."

He realized the absolute silence about him by the fact that now he heard trivial, insignificant noises. Steam-jets came on—hydrogen peroxide sprayed into a catalysis chamber where it broke down instantly into steam and gas. The product rushed out the fin-tip jets. The universe visibly turned upside down; the sky was down beyond his feet, and the singular, unfamiliar object which was Earth could be seen only when he craned his neck to look upward.

He felt no difference, of course. He'd had no weight before, and he had none now. The appearance of Earth changed so gradually that he didn't really realize that he was approaching it. But he knew it in his mind, and he resented bitterly that he had passed the high point of this achievement and was now bound back toward the commonplace, the ordinary.

He made an effort to become his normal self. "Now I suspect I'm getting scared," he said wryly into his helmet mike. If he admitted it he'd be ashamed and so could fight it. But he found that he wasn't really scared. He was apprehensive, as one is when approaching a dentist's chair. He felt reluctant, because he knew that after he got down he'd be due for ghastly, tedious days during which the doctors would go over him almost with microscopes to hunt for sputters—the burned, exploded patches that would show up where cosmic-ray particles not slowed by air went through his body. There shouldn't be any, but there could be some. Robot instruments said no sputters. But a man had to come up here to make sure.

He felt something—a featherweight of pull toward the pointed tip of the nose-cone. The rocket had hit air which slowed it enough so he noticed it. He was astounded that he'd come back so far so fast. True, he was still almost unthinkably high by the standards of other men, but he'd been out in space!

Earth was deplorably near. At twenty miles up—a hundred-odd thousand feet—the processes for landing him should begin. He settled himself in his seat against what was coming.... He suddenly realized that he'd been talking, though he didn't remember what he'd said. Undoubtedly, though, he'd said everything that came into his head. He stopped. The headphone voice said encouragingly, "You're okay!"

"So far!" he answered.

There was the story about the optimist who fell off a

skyscraper. Twenty stories earthward he saw someone looking out a window and called, "Everything's fine so far!" Yes....

There was an explosion and he started. Then others. They came from small, half-pound explosive charges set at carefully chosen places on the rocket. They were there to wreck its streamlined shape; to make it an irregular, dynamically inefficient object which would offer enormously increased resistance to its own fall through the air. Technically it was considered that the terminal speed-of-fall of the shattered rocket would be less than that of a man falling free without a parachute. What was that? A hundred and fifty miles an hour, or a hundred and twenty? McCauley tensed himself.

It seemed that something broke loose. The rocket reeled. It plunged. It turned end over end and McCauley was flung intolerably this way and that against the straps that held him in his seat. A wallop nearly snapped his neck. But this was the way it was supposed to be. Streamlined, the rocket would have struck nose-first and buried itself in small fragments in the sandy soil below. This way....

It mushed. It wabbled. It tumbled as crazily as a maple leaf and as dizzily. McCauley steeled himself to endure it. "Sixteen more miles of this!" he thought.

But it was nearly over. There was another flash of explosive, this time nearby, and the nose-cone flew violently apart and a blast of wind hit him. Then there was a thump—a terrific thump—and a no less bone-shaking bump, and his acceleration seat was ejected and he was flying free through nothingness. Then the straps miraculously came loose and he was turning end for end; Earth and sky were playing merry-go-round in all directions simultaneously, while something ungainly and monstrous writhed crazily away from him and toward the agile Earth. And then there was a jolt and a jerk and another jerk....

He swung widely, but right-side up, beneath a perfectly commonplace government-issue parachute a mere three miles high. He was sore and bruised and shaken and dizzy, but everything was perfectly all right. He'd been ejected from the falling rocket just as instruments had been ejected hundreds of times before, and an ordinary parachute had opened to let him sink tranquilly and safely to the ground, just as it had done with the instruments.

He was remarkably close to solidity now. He got his breath and saw the mountains and the vast, ridged, sun-baked, mesquite-dotted ground of the rocket site. He could see the officers'-quarters building where he'd had breakfast this morning. He spotted the blockhouse, with the spindling launching tower from which he had departed so recently.

Then he saw a trail of dust flowing across the ground below. It was the pickup gang. He'd been tracked every second, and they'd be underneath when he touched ground. Randy would be there, and the other men who'd give their eyeteeth to have taken his place. But they'd be gloating because he'd gotten back all right. They'd be grinning, swearing, exultant, overjoyed....

It suddenly occurred to McCauley that it would be intolerable if they weren't glad. He didn't feel proud himself. He hadn't done anything. He'd just gone for a ride that they'd made possible. But all the same he was filled to bursting with the goodness of what had happened.

He saw the whole thing in perspective now. Swinging below the parachute, he could estimate with fine precision just what had taken place. It had become possible for a man to go up to the edge of emptiness, to where he could look with his own eyes upon the sun and stars in their own unshielded splendor. And because a man could do it, a man had to.

And he'd been the man.

He felt overwhelmingly good as he settled, swaying, under the white blossom of nylon cloth, with the pickup gang streaking in half a dozen vehicles toward the place where he would land. Long plumes of yellow dust followed each one.

Earth came floating up to meet him.

2

(When Ed McCauley was still a reasonably young officer, there were many commonplace things that hadn't been done yet. Satellites circled the earth from west to east and across both poles and with other assorted orbits. There were artificial satellites in orbit even around the sun, and every so often somebody put up a new one for some new purpose. There'd been a landing on the moon—by robot—and a robot station there spasmodically reported temperatures and cosmic-ray frequency, and a surprising number of moonquakes.

****

But even so, many things hadn't yet been done. Man had circled the earth in capsules, but not yet had any man lifted his own rocketship from Earth and set himself in orbit. Still less had any man risen into space as the captain of his ship and brought it back to earth. Until such a thing was done, it would be absurd to speak of spaceships. Missiles, yes. Satellites, yes. But a ship had to take off and land on its own before men could say there is such a thing as a spaceship.)

Young Major McCauley arrived at Quartermain Base in an Air Transport ship which stopped briefly to drop him off and toss out a mail sack which was instantly taken in charge by two side-armed noncoms and hauled away. Then the Transport ship bellowed vociferously and took off across the incredibly level pebbly plain, lifted and retracted its wheels, and soared up into the infinitely blue sky of this part of the world. It left McCauley standing in a vast emptiness, except for unimpressive base buildings. He felt singularly lonely.

Nobody paid any attention to him. There was nobody left around. In a way it was a relief, because McCauley had experienced much too much attention once upon a time, and he wanted no more of it. He'd done a job in an Aerobee once, and now he was to try

22

something in an X-21 that a lot of people would have liked to try in his place. He preferred not to be reminded of either thing. So quite uncomplainingly he trudged across the sun-baked flat ground toward the base buildings. All around there was astounding flatness. The low hills that rose at the far side of this dry lakebed were conspicuous here, whereas in more rolling country they'd never be noticed. There was a row of hangars. McCauley picked one out with his eyes and guessed that the new ship might be inside it.

He reached the building behind the flagpole and shifted his bag from one hand to the other. He went in, mopping his forehead as the door closed behind him and the sharp chill of air conditioning hit him.

He went to report in. The CO wasn't around. He was over in Laurelton, the town where most of the men went when they got a pass. The OD was off somewhere. But quarters had been assigned to Major McCauley. The noncom in charge of the CO's office obligingly got up to show him the way.

"Any orders for me?" asked McCauley. "I don't suppose I'm supposed to sit and twiddle my thumbs."

The noncom looked at a file and said there weren't any.

"It doesn't look too lively around here," said McCauley, "I'm supposed to have an interest in the X-21. Could I take a look at her?"

The noncom did a double take.

"Oh," he said politely. "You're that Major McCauley! I should have realized it, sir. The X-21, sir, is in the big hangar down that way. Number seven. If you tell the sentry who you are he'll pass you in, sir. Of course. Take-off's tomorrow noon, sir, and everything's ready. But I'd better show you your quarters first, sir."

McCauley blinked. He felt embarrassed, and he felt a distinct sense of shock. He was embarrassed because he'd had to mention the X-21 and who he was, as if he were pushing his weight around. The shock was the take-off for tomorrow. He'd known nothing about it.

He picked up his bag and waited to be shown his quarters. He followed the noncom down silent halls with specklessly polished floors. He entered the room assigned to him. It had tan plasterboard walls and an iron bunk, and Venetian blinds to shut out the desolate outer world. It was exactly like all other bachelor officers' quarters everywhere in the world. McCauley should have felt at home. He didn't.

"Just a minute," he said carefully, as the noncom was about to leave. "You said take-off's tomorrow?"

"Yes, sir," said the noncom. "I believe it was slated for later, sir, but something came up and I understand that Major Furness—he's the general's aide, sir, besides being your observer—Major Furness assured the general that an earlier take-off would be quite all right, so the ship was checked out yesterday for fueling. The general likes things done ahead of time, sir. He says that if you do today all the things you could put off until tomorrow, you can take tomorrow off."

"Major Furness," repeated McCauley, "okayed the earlier take-off time."

"Yes, sir," said the noncom.

When the noncom closed the door behind him, McCauley burned. There can be trivial things about the feel of a ship that nobody can realize but the pilot. Certainly he should decide when an experimental ship is right to take up. He'd been denied this right. Take-off was tomorrow.

But on the other hand, he was vulnerable. He'd had a lot of publicity from that Aerobee ride he'd taken. There were a bunch of people waiting for him to put on a grand air. If he protested anything, they'd say he was putting on an act out of self-importance. So that, short of something glaringly wrong, he had to go along with a decision he hadn't made or subscribed to. He was always in danger of seeming to have a swelled head and an inflated ego and other undesirable symptoms. He needed to avoid them carefully. Right now he smoked a cigarette to kill time lest he seem overanxious to look at the X-21.

He didn't expect to be surprised by the ship. Most of the time she was building he'd been sweating out the details of the job of flying her. In Dayton there'd been a mock-up with instruments and controls in a cabin which exactly matched the ship that was not yet completed. An elaborate simulator-trainer controlled the controls and dials. When he got into the mock-up and worked it, the instrument readings, sounds, vibrations, and sensations were exactly what painstaking calculation foretold for the actual ship. It was an adaptation of the training devices that equip submarine crews to function like well-oiled machines the instant they're transferred from training to active service. It was much, much better than the dual-control planes they used to use for teaching fledgling pilots. The mock-up supplied not only the instrument readings of actual flight, but the feel of it. And not only that, it convincingly presented hair-raising emergencies. A man could experience all the griefs of a lifetime of flying in a few hours in such a mock-up. McCauley'd had them.

In the nature of things, the X-21 couldn't be given a test flight. It couldn't be tucked under a bomber's wing and lifted aloft to see how it behaved. Nothing could be done with it but take off and try to ride it where no other pilot-controlled ship had ever been, and then try to get it back down again..... If possible! If everything went well, it would be a very good job to have done. If anything went wrong, it would be too bad. Period.

McCauley smoked a second cigarette to kill time. Then he went out of his room and found his way outdoors. Squinting in the glaring sunshine, he located Hangar Seven.

Ten minutes later he was inside, taking a look at his ship. He'd hardly seen a soul along the line of hangars. Inside one he'd heard a tapping where some flight mechanic was working at something or other. From another he'd heard voices—tranquil lazy tones indicating that whoever was within had no very urgent work on hand. It appeared that practically all the base had been given a pass on the day before the shoot. Which bespoke a way of running things that meant either absolutely top management or something he'd rather not imagine.

He looked at the ship, the X-21. It was huge. It was sleek. It was impressive. It looked slightly insane, because it was built to accomplish something that most people weren't even thinking about yet. Naturally it looked improbable, like the generality of things designed to achieve the preposterous.

For one thing, the pilot's cabin was in the nose, and it hung down so the pilot could look directly behind him underneath the belly of the ship. That meant an imbalance in the wind resistance when the ship was in flight. But the balance was restored by wings above the fuselage top. Then there were enormous ramjets built into the wings well away from the body; they threw the balance off again until it was restored a second time by the wind resistance of the wheels, which did not retract. And near the tail with its triple fins there were brackets for Mark Twenty jatos, and behind them a very familiar conical bore, the exhaust nozzle of the rocket engine.

McCauley recognized everything from his preparations for flying just this ship. She would take off on jato thrust which would get her off the ground and traveling fast enough for the ramjets in the wings to catch. The ramjets would take her up to the very edge of the atmosphere. When there wasn't enough air left for even ramjets to work with, the rocket should take over. In theory the ship might be called a three-stage design, but in fact it didn't fit into any category. It did, though, have one standard property of a hydrazine-nitric rocket. If it made other than a feather-light landing with any rocket fuel remaining, it would almost certainly blow itself to blazes.

But the point was that if—if—everything went all right, McCauley ought to get up into space with a full load of rocket fuel and a few hundred miles an hour eastward velocity. On the way up he'd try to hit the jetstream at thirty thousand feet or so and pick up some speed from that. And when he started his rocket engine he was supposed to put the ship in orbit.

That was the trick. That was what had never been done before. Men had orbited in missiles and gotten down again. There was a man on the moon—or so it was believed—though he was dead before he arrived there. There were satellites circling Earth in all directions, some of them as much as ten years aloft. But nobody had ever yet sent a ship up under its pilot's control, its pilot achieving an orbit and then bringing the ship down to the surface of the earth again. When that was accomplished, it could be said that a spaceship existed. Until then, there were only missiles.

McCauley worked his way thoughtfully around the monster,

whistling soundlessly as he looked it over, checking everything he saw with what he knew, and thereby getting more information than was seemingly possible. Presently he went in the cabin and worked the controls. They felt just like the mock-up.

He was back in his quarters, thinking somberly, when there was a knock on the door. When he answered, the door was pushed open and the remarkably personable Major Furness appeared.

"Hi," he said. "They tell me you got here."

"Yes," agreed McCauley. "I did."

"They tell me you looked over the ship," said Furness exuberantly. "Good, eh?"

"It looks good," agreed McCauley.

"Were you surprised when you heard take-off's tomorrow?"

McCauley nodded reservedly.

"That's my doing," said Furness proudly. "I told the general we'd be ready. He was cussing a blue streak. An intelligence report had come through, saying that—um—there's to be an attempt abroad to lift a rocket up and set it down again on its own tail. Lift and land. No rocket's ever landed unsmashed, you know."

"I know," said McCauley.

Furness grinned. Engagingly.

"So it won't look good if us Americans get our eye wiped by somebody else doing something with a rocket that we can't do. The general made the air blue. So I said, 'General, McCauley's been training for our job for months, off there in Dayton. He's all set to do his stuff. The ship's practically ready to go. We could get it ready to take off the day after McCauley gets here. Why not do it?' And the General said, 'Furness, if we could....' And I said, 'General, we can!' So he began to give orders right and left. And that's it. Tomorrow noon. Twelve hundred. Get it over with, eh?"

McCauley opened his mouth. He closed it. Anger swept over him and he opened it a second time.

Then he shut up. For him to protest anything short of plain suicide would be considered pomposity and self-importance. But he should have had a chance to look over the ship before take-off. He'd had a glance at it, hardly more. Yet he couldn't afford to stand on his dignity or his rights because too many people envied him.

Furness looked at him and flushed a little. The cordiality that should exist between two men who are going to risk their necks together was totally missing. Furness felt it. His expression grew almost defiant.

"Look here!" he said. "That was all right, wasn't it?"

"I don't know," said McCauley. "Anyhow it's done."

Furness stared at him.

"What else was there to do?"

"I wouldn't know," said McCauley. "The ship can't be test-flown, of course—not in any ordinary sense of the word. You can't test-fly a hydrazine rocket, and among other things that's what this ship is. You just have to take it up. But—hm—how were the tests on the rocket motor?"

"They gave four per cent over the maximum expected thrust," said Furness, exuberant again. "Nothing wrong there!"

"They were cut in and out frequently?" asked McCauley.

That was one of the tricky items. A rocket motor is cut off, in a ballistic rocket, and cut in again after a pause in its firing. It isn't a sensible thing to do ordinarily, but it would be necessary in flying the X-21. It was a point about which McCauley had certain reservations. A rocket motor is very nearly a device for producing a continuous explosion, the recoil from the explosion constituting the thrust. Rocket motor design is pretty well worked out, but there are occasional failures, as in any high-precision apparatus. And the motor of the X-21 would need to cut in and out, often. It would burn fuel at the rate of more than two thousand gallons per minute. It would have to start instantly, with full pressure and full flow of two dissimilar liquids, and they would have to meet at exactly the proper spot in the rocket motor cavity and burn completely on contact. When the rocket was cut off, the fuel would have to stop flowing instantly, without the fraction of a fraction of one per cent of either liquid left unburned, or there would be trouble when the motor started again. The bare fact that the X-21's motor would have to fire and stop and fire again meant that absolute perfection was needed in all sorts of auxiliary equipment. The pumps. The fuel flow lines. There was the possibility of hydraulic hammer. There could be turbulence in the tanks because of intermittent flow.

Decidedly the motor should be tested intensively for flaws in cut-in and cut-out operation, and it should be tested in the ship and not merely in a static-thrust frame.

Furness frowned.

"I don't know what the tests were," he said with a trace of impatience. "They tested everything. They say everything's all right. I'm no reaction motor technician! I'm a pilot! They give me a ship and I fly it! I leave the other stuff to the slide-rule boys!"

"Who are plenty good," agreed McCauley, "and since the take-off's scheduled, that's that. We take off at 1200 hours tomorrow."

He had complete confidence in the adequacy of his training in the mock-up back in Dayton, but it did assume that the ship would function according to its design. He'd have preferred to verify the point he'd raised. The record of rocket shoot failures includes at least one rocket that didn't leave the launching pad because a certain valve closed three one-thousandths of a second late. It took two months to repair the damage so the rocket could be tried again. Then it worked perfectly.

Everything might have been—should have been—almost certainly had been—foreseen. But the chance of trouble was certainly greatest in the cut-in and cut-out feature that was necessary if the X-21 was to make its flight successfully.

"I'm sorry," Furness said elaborately, "that I was more concerned about meeting a situation that bothered the brass than guessing at questions you might raise. I told the general we'd be ready to take off. I'll tell him I was mistaken, that you're not ready."

McCauley grew impatient.

"Confound it, man!" he protested. "There are patrol ships taking position! The monitor stations will be alerted! There've been too many shoots called off or postponed! This one can't be postponed! I asked a question. You can't answer it. The answer would almost certainly be that there were plenty of cut-out trials. I withdraw the question. It's canceled! But it wasn't unreasonable to ask!"

Furness bit his lip.

"Just the same," Furness said sourly, "you're not satisfied that I said we'd be ready to go without asking you first. Look here! Would you rather have somebody else fly observer with you?"

"I didn't suggest such a thing," said McCauley angrily, "and it's ridiculous to think of it. No! Forget the whole business!"

"It looks to me as if you resent my action," Furness said stiffly. "I shouldn't have spoken for you without written authority. I'll try to remember, hereafter, that you're the pilot and I'm only the observer."

McCauley controlled his temper with difficulty.

"This is lunacy!" he said shortly. "The thing's settled. We take off at noon tomorrow. I'm told the ship will fly. I'm ordered to fly it. You're ordered to fly with me. That's that, so far as I'm concerned!"

Furness said as stiffly as before:

"That's quite all right with me too. I should tell you, though, that my wife wanted me to invite you for dinner tonight. The general was to be there too, for a private talk over the prospects and so on. And I've got a son who's been fairly jumping with excitement over the prospect of meeting Major McCauley, the first man ever to take off in a pure rocket and get down to ground again. But you'll hardly accept that invitation, feeling as you do. I'll say you declined because you want to get some extra sleep tonight since you intend to watch the fuel-up tomorrow."

McCauley blinked at him in amazement. Furness went out.

When he'd gone, McCauley swore to himself. This was more of the attitude he disliked, expecting him to feel self-important. It was one of the penalties of having done something that got publicity. But there was absolutely nothing he could do about it.

Certainly it had been reasonable to mention the one thing that bothered him! The X-21 would take off on jatos, ride to the limit of the atmosphere on ramjets, and have the rocket motor take over there. To get the exact course and speed he needed, he'd undoubtedly have to use the rocket engine in a series of bursts after the original acceleration run. He'd have to turn it off between times. And while an alcohol-lox rocket motor had been turned off and on in flight, no hydrazine-nitric rocket ever had been. Nobody had ever needed to. McCauley would. And the idea was hair-raising.

Rocket fuel is tricky stuff at best. In the earlier X-series ships, alcohol and lox—liquid oxygen—and in one or two cases ammonia and lox, were used in the engines. They could be jettisoned in case a dead-stick landing was necessary. But nobody in his senses would think of jettisoning nitric and hydrazine as an emergency measure. That was the pair, though, that was being used in the X-21. Their great advantage is that they do not need to be ignited. Their great disadvantage is that they become active when they are combined. McCauley had inspected the fuel delivery system and he was concerned about it. In the static runs of the ship's rocket engine everything had gone well. If all went well in space, everything would be fine. But if something didn't....

McCauley couldn't tell what would happen. His training in the mock-up hadn't included meeting that emergency, because there wasn't any way to meet it.

"If it happens," he muttered, "I'll know it because I'll hear St. Peter say, 'Hello, Ed! Come in!'"

He stirred restlessly. The light on the closed Venetian blinds was ruddy now. He found that he didn't feel hungry, but he ought to. He asked the way to the officer's mess and found that it was nearly empty. Most of the base was on leave until nine o'clock, which might be the base commandant's way of boasting that sending off the first actual spaceship on her test flight was duck soup for a well-run organization.

McCauley sat alone. There were a few other officers at dinner. Some of them nodded to him. None came over. He'd gotten a little too much publicity from that Aerobee job. Nobody would come near him lest he seem to want to shine in the reflected glory of a man who was already famous and was scheduled to become more so in the next twenty-four hours—unless he turned out to be fragments of nothing in particular out in space. He was left alone.

There was nothing to do but go back to his quarters. On the way he stopped at the newsstand and bought stuff to read.

He was very, very lonely. He was acutely conscious that he hadn't acted in the best possible way about Furness' action in speaking for him about the take-off. It was true that he should have been consulted. It was true that he hadn't intended to stand on his dignity. It was even true that he'd asked for reassurance rather than information, because the tests should have been complete. But Furness took it wrongly, and there was no way to mend the matter.

He couldn't read the stuff he'd brought. He smoked and brooded until he noticed the pile of cigarette butts he'd built up. He looked at his watch and dourly went to bed. He couldn't sleep. At long last he managed to doze off by reciting the names, capitals, and principal products of all the fifty states. He made himself so boring he went to sleep.

But when he slept he dreamed, and in the dream the ship was out of its hangar and being fueled. And McCauley dreamed that the fueling was being done all wrong. Horribly wrong. There were two tank trucks beside the ship. One was the hydrazine truck and the other the nitric. And they were pumping the two liquids into the ship at the same time. In his dream, McCauley's hair stood up straight on end. He tried to protest, but words wouldn't come. The hoses were being handled exactly as hoses at a filling station were in fueling a car. A man held each hose negligently, and from time to time squinted down past the nozzle to see how nearly full his tank was. McCauley knew that it was impossible and unthinkable, but in his dream it was both possible and plausible.

He saw bubbling, fuming nitric acid spout out of the filling tube and go splashing down on the ground. The nitric acid man looked at it stupidly as more splashed down after it. And then McCauley managed to cry out—and the dream disaster happened. The hydrazine overflowed too. It poured down....

And in his dream McCauley saw a sheet of purest fire leap up. Both trucks detonated in white-hot flame, and the ship crumpled and blew into atoms....

He found himself sitting up in his bunk, gasping, with the memory of the bubbling sounds he'd made which had waked him.

It was a good dream to wake up from. He sat up and heard small noises outside in what should have been the wholly silent night. He went to the window and tilted a slat of the Venetian blind.

The ship was out of the hangar. Men swarmed about it. Trucks towed it. It was being hauled well away from the buildings on the base. The preparations for take-off had begun. It would be a long time before fueling started, though. The ship would be towed for a couple of miles over the crunching pebbly ground, just in case something went wrong at the take-off. Then there'd have to be a checkover of everything from the tires to the wingtips to the instruments to the communication systems and the igniters for the ramjets, and so on indefinitely. Hours would be consumed in the simple final inspection. The ramjet fuel would go in. The jatos would be mounted and their circuits tested—the jatos would drop off after they'd done their stuff—Then on and on, endlessly. It would be long after sunrise before anybody began to think of the rocket fuel trucks.

He looked at his watch again. He knew he couldn't go back to sleep, but he wouldn't get dressed. He stood by the tilted slat of the Venetian blind, watching the disturbance in the moonlight go farther and farther away until it was lost in the vagueness of the partly lit plain.

He sat down, but didn't turn on the light in his room. He allowed himself one cigarette. He tried to relax, but his mind was tense. He managed a rueful grimace over his dream. That wasn't a good sign. He hadn't been worried before the Aerobee shoot, or so it seemed to him now. But in that shoot he'd had nothing to do but take a ride. Everything connected with the functioning of the rocket was somebody else's worry. Now everything was up to him.

He wondered uncomfortably how Furness felt. Probably like the devil....

With such discomfortable reflections, McCauley did not feel bright and chipper when there came footsteps outside his door and then a knock. He waited for the knock to be repeated, and then said, as if drowsily:

"What's the matter?"

"Time to get up, sir," said a noncom's voice, "if you want to watch the fuel-up of your ship, sir."

McCauley timed his pause and then said, less sleepily:

"Oh. All right. I'm awake. I'll get up right away."

He waited until the footsteps moved off. Then he swore. He'd put on an act himself. He was ashamed of being keyed up. He'd posed as a man with iron nerves, sleeping soundly before the take-off of the first ship ever to try a piloted orbital flight.

When he went out of his room he disliked himself very much.

It was an hour later, and the morning sunshine was bright, when he came out of the officers' quarters and got into the jeep that was waiting for him. Furness, he learned, was already out at the ship. The general was there too. Things were moving smoothly.

The jeep rolled over the flat ground, the picked-up pebbles making a thunderous rattling against the mud-guards and a vast plume of yellow dust trailing it.

And presently there was the ship. It was a singular spectacle—the huge, seemingly clumsy object with its dropped-down cabin shining in the slanting morning light. It seemed peculiarly isolated, out here on the featureless plain. There was nothing near it to account for its existence. Empty, board-flat ground stretched out for miles in every direction. The buildings at the base seemed tiny from here. The ship was alone like a steamer in the middle of the ocean, except that men clustered about its wheels, and there was a pickup truck that had brought ladders, and tiny dark figures swarmed over the still, glistening aluminum body.

The jeep drew near. It swung in a slightly exaggerated curve and came to a stop.

"The general's yonder," said the jeep driver, pointing.

McCauley walked over. The general faced him, and McCauley saluted.

"Ah, McCauley," the general said cordially. "You look fresh and rested."

"Yes, sir," said McCauley. He saw Furness nearby. He felt very much like a heel.

"It was a good idea to get a good night's sleep," said the general.

"Yes, sir," said McCauley.

"You've got your orders," said the general. "They give you a lot of leeway."

"Yes, sir," said McCauley.

"It's hoped you'll pass over the setup checkpoints, of course," said the general. "But the satellite watching stations will pick up your signal in any case. The main thing is to make a straight orbit. Anything short of a full twenty-four-thousand-mile course will cost you an impossible amount of fuel."

"Yes, sir," said McCauley. "I'm aware of it, sir."

It was one of the paradoxes of the flight that it would take much more fuel to make a shorter flight than a longer one. A course around the northern hemisphere, for example, not crossing the equator and the antipodes, would be extravagant in terms of the fuel required simply to stay aloft. But if McCauley established a proper orbit, he'd use fuel only to take off and to land. Landing would be as tricky a job as taking off, or even trickier. But McCauley had tried all the alternative landing processes in the training mock-up. His orders permitted him to choose the landing process himself, but it was not likely that he'd have any actual choice. The decision would be made by events.

Meanwhile there was nothing to do. McCauley stood around and watched as the general was doing. Figures moved here and there about the ship a hundred yards away. Men came up to a truck parked near it and handed in completed checklists and were given other lists to check. Once there was earnest discussion and a jeep went rushing away to the base and came rushing back, and a man took a small object over to the ship, where somebody had evidently decided that something had better be replaced. Furness avoided McCauley's eye. The whole process grew tedious. The officers, including the two who would presently fly the ship, simply stood at a distance to be out of the way and vigilantly watched men who knew what they were doing. The general had an air of vast satisfaction as matters progressed with no delays and no lack of decision at the proper level. When something is well-prepared, the commanding officer's job is finished when the action starts. The general in command of Quartermain Base had prepared things well.

The men around the ship moved away from it. They piled into personnel trucks and rolled off toward the base buildings. Other trucks came out with men in fueling suits. They took their places briskly. The hydrazine truck came up. It rolled into place as if on a railroad track, so great was its precision. The fueling crew briskly and deftly loaded the ship with its full portion of hydrazine. The tanks topped off. The truck coiled its hose and moved away.

"We'll move the ship a couple of hundred yards," said the general curtly, "before loading the nitric."

This was precaution carried to an extreme. Surely nothing could be spilled on the ground here! But to fuel the nitric from an entirely new site would make assurance doubly sure. The ship's position was shifted. The group of officers moved with it. The nitric truck came out, with a fresh crew of fuelers who loaded the nitric tank.

"Now," said the general, "you and Furness can get into your flight suits, McCauley. Then I give no more orders. You'll be on your own."

"Yes, sir," said McCauley.

A jeep came up and stopped. McCauley got in the front seat. Furness got silently into the back. The jeep raced toward the base. Crunching pebbles and raising dust, it created an extraordinary effect of self-importance and busyness.

The flight suits were in the building behind the flagpole. There were noncoms to help them don the clumsy, tight, intricately gadgeted outfits which provided protection against the effects of high acceleration, abrupt decompression, heat, cold—everything but sudden death. There were helmets. There were oxygen bottles and parachute-packs and mikes and headphones. When the two of them were completely outfitted, they looked like oversized robots.

Furness did not speak on the way back to the ship. McCauley made one half-hearted attempt to end the constraint between them.

"Isn't your wife coming out to watch the take-off?" he asked.

"She'll know when we go," said Furness without expression.

He said no more. McCauley carefully did not shrug his shoulders. But now the immediate problems of the take-off had to be thought over for the thousandth time, and he could spare no more thought for Furness' injured dignity.

They reached the standing group of officers. The ship's fuel was all aboard. The jatos were mounted. Now one man was working alone at the very tail of the ship. He was bleeding the air out of the fuel lines between the tanks and the rocket engine. He came away with a small bucket. Unlike a more normal rocket which would stand nose up and have its fuel tanks vertically above the motor, in the X-21 a certain amount of fuel had to come through the lines almost to the engine, to make certain that the pumps would deliver the two fuel elements at absolutely the same instant for self-ignition, the instant the rocket motor was turned on.

"Take that stuff," ordered the general, "and carry it well away from the ship."

A noncom ran to get the bucket. It might be nitric or it might be hydrazine. He carried it away a hundred yards or so. The lone man by the ship now stripped off his plastic coverall, including the gloves. He walked twenty yards from the ship, put on a fresh outfit, and went back to the ship. Presently he came away with another small bucket.

"Get that out of the way, too," commanded the general. He turned to McCauley. "Now, McCauley, it's all yours."

"I'd like," said McCauley, "to give the engine a one-second run. Just to make sure. I'd like everybody else away."

The general nodded. McCauley lumbered clumsily across the several hundred yards between the general and the ship. Furness started to follow, but the general said briskly:

"McCauley's right, Furness. Only one man's needed. Come along."

The general and the others moved to a position less directly in line with the body of the ship. It was a completely sensible thing to do. If he did not notice that the small buckets of bled-away fuel were closer to him and the other officers than they'd been before, he could be excused for it.

McCauley reached the ship and climbed up. He carefully inspected the instruments. Then he set the rocket timer for a one-second blast, threw off the safety, and pressed the firing button.

There was an instant, horrible bellow of a thousand dragons. The ship stirred, rolled forward—and the timer cut off the fuel supply to the rocket engine. The engine died. The ship rolled, crunching, to a stop. McCauley nodded tensely to himself. He waited.

His ears were a bit numbed by the sound, but after a time he turned to look back under the belly of the ship. There was confusion back there; the group of officers seemed agitated. There was a vast upsweep of yellow dust. And there was a hole, a crater, in the sun-baked plain. The dust was thicker and yellower above it.

Furness came trudging out to the ship. It was a good two minutes before he arrived. He climbed heavily upward and swung to close the pressure door and dog it. He settled in his seat with a thud, and then reached forward and flipped the communicator switch.

"Furness reporting, X-21 to control," he said into his microphone. "X-21 set to take off. Over."

McCauley saw that his face was ashen white.

"What's the matter, Furness?" he demanded sharply. "Anything wrong?"

"All those precautions were no good," said Furness harshly. "The stuff that bled out of the fuel lines turned over when the rocket blast hit it. It blew. It made a hole in the ground and pebbles flew every which way like bullets. One of them ripped the side of the general's cap clean off. For a moment I thought the ship had gone."

A tinny voice sounded from a speaker overhead.

"Control to X-21. Scheduled take-off time is now thirty-four seconds off. I will count down for time of take-off only." A long pause. "Twenty seconds." Another pause. "Fifteen." A silence which seemed ages long. McCauley settled himself. Furness held one hand oddly against his side. McCauley held his finger over the jato button. "Ten," said the tinny voice. "Nine ... eight ... seven ... six ... five ... four ... three ... two ... one ... take-off-ti-."

The last syllable was never completed. McCauley hit the jato button and the Mark Twenty jatos flamed, instantly and together. The jolt of the one-second blast before had been severe. This was punishment. McCauley was slammed back into his acceleration chair with intolerable violence. For two—five—seven seconds there was no world but weight and bellowings. There was nothing to be seen, nothing to be heard, nothing to be felt but the unbearable sound and intolerable pressure of the ship's acceleration.

On the outside, of course, more detailed impressions were

possible. From absolute immobility, the ship suddenly rushed forward with mountainous masses of jato fumes swirling and mushrooming behind it. The noise was deafening even at half a mile. Then the ship lifted, flying steadily and gaining velocity at a preposterous rate. Then that rate increased.

McCauley knew when it happened. For six out of their life of fourteen seconds, the jatos pushed the ship ahead at an acceleration of eight gravities; in effect, McCauley was pushed back against his chair with a force of twelve hundred pounds. Then the ramjets caught. The ship was clear of the ground, with only inertia and air resistance to hold it back. The ramjets howled, and the whole ship jerked—a little to one side as well as ahead—and then the acceleration was ten gees. The difference was that between the unbearable and the unendurable. McCauley clamped his teeth fiercely and strained to survive this monstrous assault upon his consciousness and his life.

The jatos burned out and dropped off. The ship swept on smoothly, and there were only two gees acceleration. But McCauley had to work swiftly, in spite of feeling that flatirons were attached to his fingers. He shook his head and panted, and swept his eyes around the horizon. It was level. He grasped the stick, unlocked it, and pulled it back. The horizon dipped downward before him and the ship rose tumultuously toward the sky.

He heard Furness' voice as a faint murmur above the overwhelming noise from the ramjets.

"X-21 reporting. Take-off complete. Everything functioning normally. Rate of ascent...."

His voice went on. There was a strange note in it, though. Even in his desperate absorption in the task at hand, McCauley noted it. But he could not spare a look at Furness.

The ship was airborne and already two thousand feet high. McCauley put it into a gigantic climbing sweep around a circle fully twenty miles across. It flew with the grace and precision of a garbage scow. Now and again it tended to wallow in flight, and he balanced it tensely, and then delicately as he confirmed the calculated feel of its controls.

The earth spread out below, wider and wider as the ship rose, and the ramjets thundered a message of the flight to the empty plain and all the rolling ground beyond it.

Furness' voice was barely audible. He talked steadily, reading off instrument indications into a microphone. There were telemeterings of all these data in transmission that were being recorded down at the base, but when the ship reached the limit to which the ramjets could carry it and began its rocket-powered flight, continuous reception of microwaves would be dubious. A longer wave length for a voice broadcast was necessary if the full value of the flight was to be realized.

The X-21 was eighteen thousand feet up when it passed Quartermain Base on its first circle. Half the atmosphere was already beneath it. Furness read off the fuel consumption of the ramjet.... The air speed.... The altitude. His face was as gray as when he entered the cabin. He kept his left hand pressed stiffly against the left side of his abdomen. McCauley was aware of it, but could not spare the time to think about it.

The eastward-flowing jetstream rushed invisibly overhead. That river of racing air, pouring west to east at three hundred miles an hour and better, was lower than ordinary today. The ship should hit it at twenty-eight thousand feet. McCauley had to get into it without risking the sheering stresses the bottom part of it might exert. He had to get into it like a man stepping onto a moving sidewalk. He adjusted the rate of climb. At twenty thousand feet the ramjets were more effective. The ship climbed more steeply. There was a difference in the bellowing of the ramjets. The noise was still monstrous, but it was thinner. It did not have the substance of thunder at ground level. But the sound was still so tremendous that it seemed to fill all of McCauley's consciousness. It required an effort of will to see, when he was so battered and hammered at by sound. It was difficult to think. His hands were heavy, and movements of which he would ordinarily have been unconscious now required almost painful effort.

Twenty-five thousand feet. McCauley glanced at the gyrocompass, computed swiftly in his head, added together his known air speed and the reported wind direction at this height, and deduced an actual course. Then he had to guess at the angle at which to hit the jetstream so that when its direction and speed were added to the ship's, the result of the several forces would be a course around the globe as nearly as possible the right one. It should pass over the most closely placed tracking stations, and it should not be immoderately far from the wide-spaced Navy ships which had been alerted for the flight and a possible unscheduled descent.

He swung the ship from its circling. He aimed it up and up, south-east by a half east. The ship climbed.

There was a logy wallowing when it penetrated the bottom of the jetstream. But it kept on, and presently a clock assured McCauley that he'd been in the stream long enough to gain all the extra speed it could give him. He aimed the ship's nose still higher and gave the ramjets every particle of fuel they could consume.

The sky grew dark. Dark purple. Faint twinklings appeared here and there. They were the stars, visible in daylight. The ramjets' tumult was still thinner now. And little by little the rate of climb grew less.

Presently the ship did not climb at all. It was as high as the ramjets could take it. Now the sunshine on its aluminum body was painfully bright, but the sky was almost black. Had there been time, he could have traced the constellations—the same constellations that people down below would not see for months, until this part of the heavens shone down on Earth's dark side.

In the pressurized cabin, Furness' voice was more nearly audible. But this was the first of two moments of truth. Here and now McCauley had to perform, as the act of a man, what highly complicated machines would later compute he should have done. He had to get the X-21 into a three-dimensional relationship to the gravitational field of Earth. He had to point the ship not only laterally but vertically in the exact direction that the exact timing of rocket thrust would convert into an orbit. An error of half a degree would immediately be fatal. An even smaller error could make the ship's course so eccentric that when he got back into air it would be with a velocity that would burn ship and men together as a meteor some fifty miles high.

He sweated, in absolute absorption in his task. Not only did the ship have to point exactly when he fired the rocket engine, but it had to be stationary, so it would not move past that point. It had to be settled dead center on an imaginary optimum or the rocket thrust would change direction as the ship's nose turned.

He flung his hand against a switch. The ramjets died. There was a vast, furry stillness—the deafness produced by the past din. McCauley spoke and barely heard his own voice. He shouted to Furness:

"Settle back for rocket fire!"

Furness nodded. He looked cadaverous. His eyes seemed filled with a peculiar, tragic despair. But his lips moved. McCauley knew that he was saying:

"Ramjets off. Maneuvering for course prior to rocket firing. Over."

But he did not stir in his seat. His left hand stayed pressed against his side.

The ship would be coasting downward now. Its wings still gave some support, and its wingtips had some effect, but not enough. Now was the time to use the steam-jets on the fins. McCauley played them tensely as if they were a musical instrument. He struck balances of opposing thrusts as if they were chords. The nose of the ship steadied, steadied, steadied....

The timer button was set at one minute. He struck the rocket-firing button.

He was hurled back in his seat with a sort of vicious and unreasonable violence. He was caught in a vise of twelve gravities pressure which held him motionless against the seat back and tried to flatten out his legs and body and prevent his breathing. But his flight suit was designed to prevent exactly this. It squeezed also. His legs were tightened unbearably. His arms were constricted past endurance. His chest, his stomach—he was confined in the most horrible of strait jackets. He felt his tongue curling back down his throat to strangle him. With an utterly herculean effort he managed to turn his head to one side. Then he could breathe, and the grav-pressure air protected his chest from collapse, and he endured and endured and endured.

The minute of the rocket thrust lasted for centuries. Then the engine cut off, and his head was pure anguish from the blood spurted through it by his still-laboring heart. He was blinded by the pain. But it went away.

Slowly, slowly, slowly, his sound-deadened ears regained their sensitiveness. He heard Furness gasping:

"—minute rocket-blast ended. Checking course now. Over."

McCauley said absorbedly:

"There was a goof. A twelve-gee thrust with full fuel tanks is a whale of a lot more when they're nearly empty!"

It was true, of course. The ferocity of a rocket thrust that would accelerate a fully loaded ship at three hundred fifty-odd feet per second per second would accelerate much more a ship weighing half as much. Toward the end, McCauley and Furness had taken acceleration that no man could live through for more than a very short time. But a man can endure briefly a stress that would kill him if long-continued.

McCauley plunged into the desperately necessary task of this moment. He had to determine his present course and speed. He could not take the time to look out of the ports at the immensity of Earth below him. Men in capsules, orbiting, had been as high as this, but they did not have to compute their height or guide their vehicles. McCauley had to do both.

The height was relatively simple. A radar screen, reduced to a vertical slot for economy of space and weight, told him the distance to whatever was below. A Doppler-effect velocity indicator would read off the change in frequency of a crystal-controlled radio signal which his speed produced. This substantially resembled the way an automobile horn changes pitch when two cars pass each other; the pitch drops swiftly at the moment of passing. But there was an observation which was simpler and more direct.

He spotted a bright star near the horizon ahead. He read off its angular distance from the world's edge. Looking aft, under the belly of the ship, he read another angle from the world's edge to another star. Minutes later, he repeated the observations. The star ahead was higher, the one behind was lower. If one star rose faster than the other sank, he would be gaining height. If one sank faster than the other rose, he would be falling. If one rose exactly as fast as the other dropped, he would be in a perfect circular orbit, neither rising nor falling. That was too good to be expected. But from even two sets of observations he could tell the line the ship was following, and hence its speed.

The ship did not have quite the speed necessary for a complete orbit. It needed more. He could guess how much.

He said curtly to Furness:

"We've got to have a two-second push, anyhow. Maybe more later. Get set."

Furness did not reply, but McCauley heard him reporting.

There was singularly little exultation in the small cabin. Furness' face was drawn and colorless behind his helmet plate. McCauley was busy.

Presently, after a warning gesture, he set the rocket timer and pressed the firing button. All the ghastly impact of high acceleration repeated itself. But, lasting only two seconds, it was not much worse than—say—falling from a second-story window down on a hard mattress. It lasted longer, but there was not much other difference. It did not build up to the torture of continued rocket thrust.

Then the ship floated on. There was utter silence. The vertical-slot altimeter indicated a height which seemed absolutely steady. The Doppler-effect velocity meter gave a reasonably satisfactory if not too precise message. McCauley was working intensively on his course when Furness said, with an effort:

"Ground says satellite-watching stations picking up our signal report a good course. It could be a little more to the south."

McCauley flipped on his own microphone-to-ground switch.

"I figure I'm still a little short on velocity," he said crisply. "I'll have to blast again for about a second. Figure me an angle of heading for ten minutes from now, for a one-second blast. I'll report my figures for checking."

He did not bother with the ship controls now, of course. The ship was in orbit, like the numerous satellites circling Earth west to east and north and south. It did not matter which way it pointed. There was no air to impede its progress. As a matter of fact, a trace of rotating motion had been produced by a slight off-centering of the rocket thrust. The ship's center of mass had changed slightly because of fuel consumption.

There was silence. McCauley worked on busily. From time to time Furness spoke as if with great effort. He relayed the altitude from the slot radar. He relayed the velocity from the Doppler gauge. He relayed hull temperature, cosmic frequency, ultraviolet intensity. He did not report any physical sensations, but once he spoke as if in answer to a question:

"It must be out of order if it says that."

He might be referring to the telemetering apparatus which relayed the pulse and respiration and blood pressure readings of the two men in the ship.

In eight minutes McCauley reported the bearing he considered the ship should point to so that a one-second rocket thrust, adding its effect to all previous courses and speeds—plus a correction for the diminished weight of fuel in the tanks—would produce an exactly perfect orbit for the ship. Furness repeated it while McCauley took more horizon-to-star observations to check the present line of motion.

"Ground checks your figures," said Furness. "They say congratulations on perfect astrogation under service conditions. It's right."

"Okay," McCauley said absently.

He went on with his work. The ship was two hundred eighty miles—plus or minus half a mile—above the surface of the earth. An orbit required a speed and rate of downward curvature just fixed so the ship would go downward as the surface curved down, like a glider coasting down a curving hillside and always being the same distance from solidity. Since the earth was a globe, one could coast forever and be always falling, without ever touching the circled world. That is an orbit.

McCauley set the rocket timer and said:

"Here we go."

The rockets blasted. The ship flung itself forward. Again there was the sensation of falling an uncomfortable distance onto a hard mattress. But a one-second blast was a thousand times more endurable than a one-minute one.

The ship had now been aloft for something like thirty minutes, of which ten was airborne flight and twenty free fall in orbit, plus two corrections of course and speed. McCauley had had no time to gaze down at the vastness below him. He knew it only as a huge expanse of mottled tawny-green or blue with many white specks upon it. The specks, which were clouds, were closer together toward the horizon, and at any given moment the rim of the world was a ring of plain white.

Now he checked his work once more and then took time to look at Earth below him. At its speed, the ship should complete one revolution of the Earth in ninety minutes, more or less. Its speed was seventeen thousand two hundred and sixty miles per hour relative to the ground. In twenty minutes of free-fall flight it had covered something over five thousand and seven hundred miles, relative to the ground, and crossed eighty degrees of longitude. The local time down below was something more than five hours later than the local time at Quartermain Base. Sunset would be approaching here, as the earth's shadow moved from east to west like the dawn.

To the right of the floating ship there was only tawny-blue ocean that seemed much darker than ordinary because McCauley was looking down into its depths instead of at a sky reflection from its surface. Behind the ship there was a clumping of the white specks. These cloud masses would be above and around the Cape Verde Islands, now tens of scores of miles to the rear. Below and to the left there was an amorphousness, an indefiniteness peeping up from beneath the cloud cover. That would be Africa. McCauley could see for enormous distances over the cloud-hidden land. He knew that he floated over Senegal and British Guinea and French Guinea and Liberia and the Ivory Coast, all in a matter of tens of seconds. But he could see only at intervals between tufts of white-cottony vapor. Ahead, too, the dark-colored sea swept in, right to left, and in half minutes or less there was no land at all except behind him. Away ahead there was more of Africa, to be sure, because the X-21 sped along a line which would mark the limits of the Gulf of Guinea. The ship would cross the tip of Africa and head down past it to Antarctica.

But McCauley would not see Africa again. The whiteness which was the horizon turned dim where the ship's bow aimed, and the dimness spread to the left. The edge of the round world turned black. It was Earth's crawling shadow creating night. Darkness sped toward the ship, still high above the last slightest trace of atmosphere and glittering intolerably in the unshielded glare of the sun.

"It looks like we're all set, Furness," McCauley said with satisfaction. "We can relax, now, for all of twenty minutes."

Furness did not answer. There was no sensation of weight, of course. Nothing weighed anything. Nothing could be considered light or heavy. The difference between a copper penny and the ship itself was purely imaginary. They had different masses, but both would weigh the same—zero. McCauley suddenly turned off the silent air-circulator in the cabin. He struck a match. The flame flared, but not as a rising leaf shape. It was a perfect ball of incandescence. But it did not continue to burn. It went out, and there was a ball of white smokiness where the flame had been.

"I've heard that'd happen. I wanted to try it," McCauley said amusedly.

A match requires oxygen in which to burn. On the ground, the chemically fostered first flame of the match-head heats the air, which rises and is replaced, whereby fresh oxygen reaches the place of combustion and supports it. But in the X-21, in free fall, hot air was no lighter than cold. It did not rise. The match exhausted the oxygen around it and went out. McCauley turned the air-circulator on again lest he and Furness be similarly surrounded by vitiated air.

"Queer, eh?" said McCauley. Then he looked at Furness. Furness' eyes seemed filled with suffering. His pallor was deathlike.

"What's the matter?" McCauley asked.

Purely by instinct he raced his eyes across the instruments. They said nothing they should not.

"Furness!" snapped McCauley. "What's the matter? What's happened to you?"

With an air of terrible effort—though nothing weighed as much as a hair—Furness moved his left hand away from his side. It came away filled with blood. There was an ominous dark-red patch on the flight suit, and something seemed to be welling slowly out of a puncture in the cloth. The hole was the size of a bullet hole.

"Just before ... take-off," said Furness thinly, "the rocket fuel that was ... bled through the fuel pipes ... went off when you tested ... the engine. It exploded. It threw pebbles like bullets. One ... ripped the general's hat. One ... hit me."

McCauley swore. He felt a sort of bitter anger. Of all the places where instant medical attention for an injured man was impossible, the worst was the close, air-tight cabin of a ship out of atmosphere, traveling at some thousands of miles per hour and heading into night. Descending was out of the question. It was impossible to turn back.

"Let's look at that," said McCauley harshly. "Maybe we can check the bleeding somehow.—Why didn't you report you were hurt? Didn't you know you were risking your life?"

"I suppose," said Furness weakly, but with irony, "that you aren't risking yours!"

Then he winced a little as McCauley's finger explored the hole in the tough cloth. When the rocket fuel exploded on the surface of the ground, the impact of a pebble would have the effect of a bullet. It would numb more than it hurt. Furness knew he'd been hit, of course, but the ship was ready to take off, and the wound might only be trivial. To delay take-off for examination of what might be entirely insignificant would earn him McCauley's contempt—or so Furness had believed. And Furness was in no state of mind to risk that. Nothing short of absolute inability to hide his injury would have made him admit that he'd been hurt or even hit. So he'd climbed in the ship, and done his work steadily until this instant, all the time covering the wound with his hand lest McCauley discover it.

There was no room in the cabin for much movement. McCauley tried to enlarge the hole, but the cloth was reinforced with wire and could not be torn. Furthermore, he had nothing to work with if he could get at the wound—nothing for bandages, nothing to check the bleeding, nothing.... He swore deeply.

Then he felt for a familiar iron ring and pulled it. A tiny pilot chute leaped from his chute-pack. It was designed to pull out his main chute if he had to jump. He tore at it with his fingers.

"We'll pack it anyhow," he mumbled as he ripped strips from the small expanse of nylon. "At least check the bleeding."

He rolled up a strip of white cloth. He was irritated by the insistent feeling that he needed antiseptics he didn't have. He worked at the recalcitrant opening in the cloth of the flight suit and packed the wound with nylon. Then he worked more nylon about and over the packing to make a firm pad. He tore long strips to put around Furness' body to hold the packing fast and tied them tightly.

It was awkward to work where there was no weight. It seemed unreal to attempt the preposterous where there was no sound. He worked swiftly. Suddenly there was a redness in the light reflected all about the cabin from the sunshine that came in the ports.

He jerked up his head, thinking foolishly of fire. Then he saw the sun. It lay beyond a vast curved barrier that shut off all the light of all the stars. The sun was in the act of descending, to be eclipsed by the edge of Earth, and its light came through hundreds of miles of thick air which turned it from a burning golden glare to flame-red, and then crimson, and then ruby-red as he stared. Then its rim was blanked out and it slid swiftly down to extinction. The light went from gold to carmine to ruby and the sun was blotted out in less than ten seconds.

Then the ship traveled through purest night. The cosmos outside its ports was sharply divided. There was a hemisphere filled with the coruscations of a million million stars. The other half of the universe was the night side of Earth, but it looked like the abyss of nothingness from which all things came, and to which it may be that all things will return.

McCauley reached over and switched on lights. Furness looked at him through eyes that seemed deep-sunk in his head.

"You tore your pilot chute," he said thinly. "You've no chance to jump, now."

McCauley scowled. There were various methods by which the ship could be landed or at least its occupants might escape its crash. There was the skip process, in which the ship could be settled down into atmosphere just thick enough to slow it as it bounced out to space again for another settling, another slowing, another bounce. It was considered the most practical way for a ship to get back to Earth after an orbital flight. To choose the final landing place, of course, was out of the question. Also it was believed that even with the best of luck the ship's crew might have to take to their chutes and let the ship crash. But Furness could not make a chute-drop. Nor could McCauley, now.

"Time for a report," said McCauley.

He'd meant to make it, but Furness summoned all his strength. He ran his eyes along the instruments.

"X-21 reporting," he said as loudly as he could. "Just passed darkness line. Altitude...."

He went through the list of readings to be given by voice. They might be picked up by satellite-tracking stations which did not quite pick up the ship itself. They would almost certainly be picked up by South African radio amateurs listening for them.

"More comfortable?" McCauley asked gruffly.

Furness moved his head in a fashion that might be considered a nod. After a long time he said:

"Is there any ... water in the ... survival kit?"

McCauley fumbled. There was. The survival kits were the small parcels which might conceivably mean the difference between dying and not dying if a man had to ditch his disabled plane or jump from a burning one. Together with an inflatable boat, they were included in the X-21's equipment as a sort of pious wish. It was not to be believed that this ship would end its career like a mere atmosphere plane. If the steam-jets didn't work, the most perfect operation of the rocket engine would never get the ship down into the atmosphere, even for destruction. If it got down to the atmosphere there were still several thousand things that could go wrong. It was definitely not likely that its crew could jump to safety in case of need, or land so serenely on water that a rubber raft would do them any good. But the survival kits were there.

McCauley gave Furness water. He did not comment on the complications Furness' injury added to a landing problem that was already complicated enough. Instead, he looked at the clock.

"We're close to Antarctica now," he observed. "We ought to run into moonlight, too."

He peered out of a port. The tiny lighted cabin swam in emptiness, without sound, without sight of anything but remote and indifferent stars. It floated above the part of the world where the Indian and Atlantic Oceans flow together, and where there is unbroken sea all around the antarctic continent. A wind can blow completely around the world there, and rather frequently it does; and the gigantic waves that are engendered are spoken of with aversion by seamen. But McCauley could not see any waves. There was floating ice below, but as he thought of it it changed to the massive ice sheet of the bottom of the world. So the tiny lighted cabin raced over mountains and plains all buried in snow which had been there since the beginning.

He turned from the sight of a universe divided into stars and blackness. There was no practical measure to be taken—not now, anyhow. McCauley might contrive a way to get himself safely down to earth, letting Furness take his own chance with no strength to help himself. It seemed improbable in the extreme that Furness could survive a crash landing, even if no explosion followed. There was very little hope that the X-21 could be landed save in a crash. But it did not occur to McCauley that he was relieved of responsibility. A normal landing was not really hoped for. If McCauley piloted the X-21 into orbit and out again, he'd have done the unprecedented and the next try might go better. But he could not imagine himself leaving Furness in a ship headed for a landing that was bound to be a pile-up....

He couldn't expect to land intact himself, with his pilot chute ripped out and torn apart.

"I'm sorry you tore up your pilot chute," said Furness. "It about kills your chance of getting down to the ground in one piece. And it's my fault. You tore it up for me. But when I came on the ship I didn't think I was hurt badly."

"I'd have done just what you did," said McCauley. "It would have taken two broken legs to keep me from walking over as if nothing had happened to me." Then he remembered. "Report?"

Furness gathered his strength and spoke in an almost natural voice:

"X-21 reporting. We are over Antarctica at the farthest south part of our orbit. Altitude...."

He went through the list, and then his eyes went to the canteen from which McCauley had given him water. McCauley gave him another drink.

"That son of mine," said Furness abruptly. "He reveres you. When I was picked to ride observer with you, he almost went out of his head with pride. I was—I suspect I was a little bit jealous of you. A man likes his son to think he's the greatest man on earth. My boy almost believed it when I was picked for this job. But if I'd backed out...."

McCauley nodded.

"Under the circumstances," he agreed, "you'd walk to the ship and come aboard if you had to carry your head in your hand. A man wouldn't disappoint his son."

"He'd have been so proud," said Furness, "if we'd made it! And I've messed it all up!"

"I'm hanged if I'll compliment you," McCauley said, "but it would have been disgraceful if you'd done anything else. A man has to set an example for his son. And we may make out. In any case we're just thirty-two minutes from some very tricky stuff. I think we'd better think of cheerier things."

"Sorry," said Furness. He turned his eyes away. He brooded.

Seconds ticked by in the cabin. Frost began to form on the ports. There was no air outside, so there could not be said to be any temperature. But the ship radiated heat into empty space and received next to none in return. If allowed to cool until thermal equilibrium with its surroundings was reached, the X-21 would go down to some two hundred and fifty-four degrees below zero centigrade. But that would be in darkness. In sunlight it would be a different matter, and the ship'd be out of darkness in minutes.

They were very long minutes. The altitude radar said that the ship was maintaining the most nearly perfect circular orbit any man-made object had achieved to date. The X-21 was a lonely mote with yellow light glowing from its cabin openings. From time to time, invisibly, radio waves spread out from a stiff metal rod pointed sternward, and some of them might—with luck—be picked up by somebody. But the ship received nothing, here.

It passed south of Kerguelen Island in the blackness, and it was midnight local time, though the ship was only forty-five minutes of free-fall flight from Quartermain Base. Presently the X-21 headed northward and crossed the meridian where it was one A.M. something less than five minutes later. It reached a point south of Australia in under ten minutes more. It swept above the lowermost part of Australia and Tasmania together when the clocks on the ground said five A.M.

It was only when the remotest rim of the blackness which was Earth turned bright—when the dawn could be seen at the farthest horizon—that McCauley thought to look for the moon. It shone down coldly, but it was not bright enough to show him any pattern in the blackness nearly three hundred miles below the ship.

In eight minutes more, however, the sun had rolled up over the edge of the world and below the ship there was ocean. Away off to the left McCauley could see spiral arms of cloud, signifying a cyclonic disturbance moving north across the Coral Sea. Sturdy steamships fought for their lives in that typhoon, and many human beings would die in it. The ship sped on, and there came into the headphones of both McCauley and Furness a beamed message from the naval installation at Guam, which dimly and fugitively could be sighted under an aggregation of white clouds more dense than ordinary. The message said:

"Good work, guys! We're pulling for you!"

Then the Samoan Islands were far behind and dropping even farther. And time passed, and McCauley thought intensively and very grimly, and once again Furness asked for water. There was a clumping of cloud masses underneath and to the east which was Phoenix Island, and almost immediately afterward Washington Island and then Palmyra; after that it seemed barely seconds when a most respectable massing of clouds to the left was Hawaii.

McCauley could see solid ground there, and he talked curtly and very urgently into his own throat-mike, flipped into circuit with the voice transmitter for the occasion. It was not altogether likely that his message, relayed, would arrive ahead of the ship, but it was his only chance to do anything practical in the way of warnings to the ground.

He set to work. He did computations from instrument readings he barely remembered. He included a prayerful hope that the fuel-gauge instruments had been calibrated through their entire range. There was so much ramjet fuel, which might or might not do what it was supposed to do. There was so much rocket fuel, which must be expended to the last smallest drop before the ship could risk touching ground. And there was distance to be calculated, in terms of minutes and seconds instead of miles.

The clock flashed a red light and made a buzzing sound. It was a reminder that now, according to the figure evolved on the ground before take-off, McCauley might begin the attempt at skip landing, the improbable but still least implausible procedure for getting the ship on to the ground in not more than two or three pieces. It should begin with a rocket-driven dive into the atmosphere. He was expected to have enough fuel for that. With downward velocity established, he should bleed out all the remaining nitric acid to emptiness. After it had been completely expelled, and not before, he should wait the number of seconds which would be equivalent to five hundred miles, and then jettison the hydrazine. By that time the ship should hit the outermost fringes of air. He should dive into it until the ship's skin temperature began to rise—a matter of fractions of seconds—and then let the ship bounce out again. It would have lost some velocity and would no longer be capable of remaining in an orbit. So it would come down into the air again, after an interval in which it would cool off, and again it would bounce out like a stone skipping across the surface of a pond until it has lost enough speed to settle quietly to the bottom.

If McCauley attempted such a landing system, his place of entry into the air for a dead-stick landing would not be less than one thousand miles from the point of the first bounce, and it might be three thousand. It could not be calculated. Fractions of seconds and seconds of arc would apply, so McCauley might start his skip-stop descent out above the Pacific Ocean, and the X-21 might finally ditch in the Atlantic somewhere off Newfoundland.

Furness tried to speak.

"Report," he said faintly. "I should report."

McCauley threw the switch for him. Furness summoned what seemed to be his last reserve of strength.

"X-21 reporting," he said almost naturally. "We are well past Hawaii and approaching the continent. Altitude...."

He was halfway through when green solid ground with very few clouds lay directly below, and the Rocky Mountains were a little way ahead. He could not quite detect their height, but the pattern of the soil was distinctive. McCauley flipped on his own throat-mike and said:

"I interrupt. Here is the situation. My fuel tanks read...." He snapped off the readings. "I'm going to swing the ship end for end and burn my remaining rocket fuel to kill velocity. Then I'll adopt such skip-stop practices as the situation requires. I doubt it will require them. We were lucky enough to get a nearly circular orbit. In consequence our velocity is lower than if we'd had to make an eccentric one. We saved fuel unexpectedly in getting into space, and I'm going to use it getting out. Over."

He cut off and made his preparations. His figuring was extremely close. But there had necessarily been a slight margin of fuel. A circular orbit does not require nearly the fuel expenditure that an elliptical one does. But McCauley had made the most efficient possible use of fuel at the beginning. He'd used one long blast, a two-second blast, and a one-second rocket thrust to get into nearly a perfect space trail. He meant to collect for that partly accidental expertness. But he meant to collect much more for an observation.

The observation was that a one-second blast was not a thousandth the ordeal that a sixty-second blast was. No man could survive a long-continued twenty-gravity acceleration. But most men could take a one-second push—and not only once, but many times. With time for recovery in between, and a rocket engine that fired infallibly when it was turned on....

He set the rocket timer.

"This," he said over his shoulder, "may be our last chance to exchange compliments, Furness. But I think you're the same kind of idiot as I am. I'd have come on this trip with my insides hanging out rather than stay behind. So would you. Very nearly, you did. It's nice to have known you. I hope we survive."

Steam-jets spouted at the ends of the X-21's rear fins. In emptiness, the ship spun halfway about until the swiftly moving solidity below ceased to move toward the pointed nose. It fled away. The ship traveled backward where there was no air.

"And here we go," said McCauley.

The rocket timer was set. He pressed the blast button. A second later he came out of near-unconsciousness and set it again. There was another rocket blast. He almost recovered from the effect of it before he set the timer for a third.

Doggedly he set the timer and pressed the button, and allowed himself three full breaths and set it and pressed again. The shocks seemed to become more and more violent and intolerable. They were. With loss of mass, the acceleration of the lightened ship went up to twenty-two gees. He cut the blasts to three-quarters of a second. A rocket cannot be throttled down. It fires full blast or it has no appreciable effect at all.

Quartermain Base was built on a flat, flat plain that extended miles in every direction. Its buildings, from a reasonable distance, were only toy structures, tiny angular objects in the middle of vastness. Overhead there was a sky of absolute blue. It was empty. Below, there was flatness to the horizon. It contained nothing. There was no motion of any sort anywhere. The base lay still and silent under the baking two-o'clock sun. Nothing happened. Nothing....

No. Something was happening. Specks moved out of the miniature buildings. Dots rolled out of the infinitesimal garages. The dots and the specks seemed to mill about uncertainly and then to come to a restless, not-quite stillness. It seemed that something was expected to happen. But there was nothing that could. There was only a great emptiness and a great stillness....

But then there came a faint roaring. It was very faint indeed. It strengthened, and diminished, and strengthened again.

Then a mote appeared in the sky. It came down and down and down, bellowing. The bellowing was the unmistakable sound of ramjets. And the thinnest of high-pitched sounds arose from the specks which were men outside the buildings at the base. The sounds were howls of triumph, shrieks of rejoicing, of gladness that the impossible had been accomplished.

The X-21 came wabbling down out of the sky and leveled off a bare hundred feet above the pebbly plain. It lowered, and lowered, and suddenly yellow dust spouted furiously where its wheels had touched. The roaring cut off. The ship rolled and rolled. Later, it would develop that less than one quart of ramjet fuel remained to be burned before it hit ground.

Shouting, swarming men rushed toward it. Dots which were trucks and cars raced to greet it.

Presently McCauley saluted very formally, standing before a general whose cap was badly ripped on one side.

"Sir," he said, "it looks like we did it. And I'd like to say, sir, that I am very proud to have had Major Furness with me. He's hurt, sir, as I radiocd to Hawaii. The ambulance is rushing him to hospital. But he stuck to his job throughout, sir, and I'll be obliged if you'll tell his son that he should be very proud of his father."

3

(Time passed after Ed McCauley became Major Ed McCauley, and most people forgot him. If his name was mentioned, someone might say vaguely: "McCauley ... McCauley? It seems to me I've heard the name." This was because remarkable events don't stay remarkable as time goes past. There was a two-hundred-pound satellite circling the moon these days, industriously sending back not only pictures of the moon's far side, but pictures of cloud masses on Earth which told much more about Earth's weather than had been known before. A drone missile had gone out to Mars, and its instruments suggested that men had better not come out just yet, and other drones had gone past Venus and said definitely that men better not come out just yet. So something had to be done to make those journeys possible. Men had to work in space, testing this and trying that, staying days or weeks at a time when solar flare-particles were not too much in evidence. This meant that there had to be a place for them to live and work. There were plenty of men who'd done spectacular things lately, but this needed somebody who would be worrying not about fame, but about getting a job done right. So Major McCauley received certain orders.)

***

On as much of the Space Platform as existed so far, a working day lasted an hour and forty minutes. There wasn't much of the Platform, as yet. The greatest bulk was a squat, clumsy metal object which had come up from Earth, pouring out rocket flames, to be the Platform's nucleus. From it now sprouted spidery, flimsy metal girders which reached out in apparent aimlessness. They formed an incomplete skeleton of joined triangles whose final form seemed indefinite. But in time they would form a most unlikely icosahedron traced in threads of silvery metal in emptiness.

58

Although the Platform was barely begun, it grew noticeably as time went by, even though the working day was so brief.

Some people would have challenged the word "day." There was no true night where the first part of the Platform floated hurriedly in orbit some three thousand miles out from the planet Earth. There was light when the sun shone on it, which was two hours and five minutes out of three hours and seven. Despite Luna, Earth's ancient and untidy moon, there was abysmal darkness when the Platform plunged into Earth's shadow. This was not nightfall. When sunlight ended, cut off by Earth's eight-thousand-mile bulk of stone and metal, the phenomenon was an eclipse. Once in each revolution about the world which was building it, the Platform was eclipsed by Earth. When light returned, it was not sunrise, it was the ending of an eclipse.

McCauley was in charge of the Platform's construction crew, which consisted of himself—a major—and Randy Hall—a captain— and Sammy Breen, a second lieutenant in the Space Service. They lived after a fashion in the cabin of the ship that had brought them and a lot of building material up and out to the orbit the Platform was to follow. When a work period ended, they made their way painfully to that cabin. They made sure that they were inside it before the sun touched the outer limits of Earth's atmosphere and turned orange and deep-red and then disappeared, all within ten seconds. It was necessary, for in Earth's shadow the gossamer-like framework lost heat rapidly. Long before the end of the eclipse, the temperature of the bare metal dropped incredibly. Even with Earth nearby to temper it, it fell to something like two hundred and twenty-odd degrees below zero.

So between work periods there was darkness and unthinkable cold, and half the universe was brilliant stars—sometimes the moon was visible—and the other half looked like a hole in emptiness leading to nowhere. Actually, the seeming abyss was the night side of Earth, and sometimes Randy or young Lieutenant Breen used the telescope and found infinitesimal twinklings on it which could be calculated to be London, or New York, or Paris, or some other metropolis. But the night lights of cities on Earth were not remarkably bright, from three thousand miles out in the planet's shadow. Often, too, there were clouds thick enough to mask any man-made illumination. There was not much to see from the Platform in darkness and at an early stage of its construction.

But after the darkness there came light.

It was not dawn, of course. It began as a reddish-pinkish line which precisely outlined a half circle and formed a visible boundary between absolute blackness and the firmament of stars. The line thickened at its ends and then at its center. Instantly thereafter the sun peered—deep-red—around the edge of the planet Earth. It was a very lively sun. In seconds it reversed the color changes of its disappearance, fading from ruby to gold and then to the furnace-flame color it shows out of the atmosphere. And the crescent of lighted Earth grew broader and broader and suddenly seas and continents and oceans and islands seemed to come pouring out to cover the darkness, like creation happening as a flood.

Then, while the partially built Platform swept onward, without sound or sensation of movement, nothing else happened for a certain time. The three men inside the cabin waited for the metal to warm up from the temperature of liquid air. During full sunshine it went up to the temperature of low-pressure steam. When all the framework was warm enough so it was no longer brittle, the cabin air lock opened. McCauley came out in a silvery space suit. Captain Randy Hall followed him. Lieutenant Sammy Breen came last. McCauley surveyed the framework. Even a tiny meteorite could do damage, because any such object could be expected to hit at a velocity of seven to forty miles per second.

But when his inspection was over, McCauley slung a space rope around a girder, straddled the metal beam, and pulled himself effortlessly along to its first triangular junction with the other frame members. He had no weight. Nothing had any weight. One could not fall from the Platform, but one could very easily become lost from it. McCauley had acquired a certain fanatical concern about precautions against loss of contact with the only object within some three thousand miles which would let a man go on living.

When he reached the first junction of frame members, McCauley unlooped his space rope from behind the junction, looped it again beyond the joining place, and crawled over to straddle the next girder and slide along it with equal absence of effort until he arrived at the place where he'd left off work a little over an hour before. Randy Hall and Sammy Breen, meanwhile, emulated him, going in other directions. Within five minutes of coming out of the air lock they were perched at three separate places on the absurd framework.

With quite inadequate-looking cords they drew large metal beams toward them from their place beside the cabin. McCauley, for example, pulled at a thirty-foot girder with a piece of string. It stirred and shifted and floated to him. He stopped it, his knees holding him fast. Then—very clumsily because of its mass—he maneuvered it into place, slipped bolts through the ready-drilled holes, and tightened up the nuts. He finished his first girder. Randy completed his. Sammy Breen got his section in place, and then stopped.

"Major, sir," said his voice via space phone in McCauley's helmet phones, "there's something wrong here. A bolt doesn't go all the way through its hole. It won't force. The hole needs to be reamed out."

It was a trivial but annoying happening. The parts for the Space Platform had been cut out, shaped, and drilled on Earth. In theory they should fit perfectly together in space. But somebody had scamped on an inspection job and the result of his carelessness had to be repaired. It had to be done in a nondescript, crazy framework that was hurtling along in orbit at something over eleven thousand five hundred miles an hour. It shouldn't have happened.

"Memorize the part number for report," said McCauley, "and get the reamer and clear it."

"Yes, sir," said Breen.

McCauley pulled gently at a cord and a second girder stirred and floated gently toward him.

Below, the sunlit surface of Earth had an extraordinary appearance. It was some sixty-five degrees in diameter. At its edges the shapes of land and water—the planetary markings—were foreshortened and crowded together in an unparalleled fashion. A twelve-inch globe looked at from five inches away will give something of the same effect. From one side of the disk the markings moved toward the center, thickening and taking recognizable form as they neared the middle. Then they went on, distorted in a different fashion as they approached the opposite edge. When McCauley set his second beam in place a wildly twisted Isthmus of Panama appeared out of the misty whiteness which bordered Earth from where he floated. In half an hour it would be directly underneath and plainly recognizable. In another half hour it would be a new shape entirely. Then it would vanish. Only the center of the visible disk resembled any map-maker's representation, and that spot changed and changed and changed as the Space Platform hurtled past. At any given moment McCauley could see a ninth of all the planet's surface, but only a fraction of what he saw was familiar, and that changed continuously.

Sammy Breen slid along the Platform's frame to the cabin, the ship which had risen to this place from Earth, but would never return to Earth again. Arrived at the cabin, he seized a handrail, loosened his space rope, and pulled himself to the air lock. Immediately, of course, air would flow into the lock and he could emerge into the cabin's interior. He'd get the tool he needed for a job that should have been done on Earth. Then he'd come out again.

Randy tapped on the girder he'd just bolted into place. The vibrations passed through the metal and through McCauley's space suit to the air within it.

"I just happened to think," said Randy cheerfully, "that people down on Earth are all excited about this thing we're building. They think it's wonderful. And so it is, at the present moment. But I'm thinking that in a little while it won't be wonderful. It'll be old stuff. And the day'll come when it's a nuisance. There'll be complaints that it's in the way, barging around through space. It'll be in the way of ships taking tourists on week-end trips to Mars. They'll say it's a danger to astrogation. They'll say it should be cleared out of space. They'll insist that it be junked."

McCauley grunted. Randy was probably right. But just now McCauley held himself to a three-by-five-inch hollow metal beam, with a million million stars shining in all possible colors at the same time as the sun. He continued to work on, building the Platform that some day would be considered a nuisance. Three thousand miles away, geographical features squirmed and twisted themselves in their progress across the disk of Earth.

"But there'll come a time," said Randy cheerfully, "when one of my twenty-five-times-removed great-grand-sons will be spanked by his mother. He'll howl. It will be a very commonplace sort of happening. The only thing odd about it will be that it won't happen down on old Earth below us. It'll happen off somewhere on a planet that nobody's dreamed of yet, circling a sun that nobody's bothered to name, off yonder somewhere in the Milky Way."

McCauley grunted again.

"You haven't any kids yet, let alone great-great-grand-kids. You're not even married. Why the sentiment?"

Randy's voice came clearly in the helmet phones.

"I've been trying to think of a reason for me to be here," he explained, "playing with an oversized Erector set, instead of chasing some girl down on Earth. And I realized that this Platform, which will eventually be junked, has to be built before we can hope to colonize the nearer planets, let alone the stars. So now I know why I'm here. I'm doing this so my many-times-removed great-grandchildren can get their spankings all over the galaxy instead of only on the insignificant earth below. That's a noble purpose! I feel better."

"Good!" said McCauley, with irony.

He felt metallic clankings through the girder on which he was working. He turned his head within the space helmet. Sammy Breen had come out of the air lock, guiding himself by a handrail to a position astride a beam. He slid swiftly along its length. He came to a junction, flipped his space rope around to the far side of the joining place, swung over, and slid to the next junction like someone coasting down a stair rail. He was a cheerful young man, Sammy Breen.

"Sammy," said McCauley, "hold everything. I'll be over."

When people encounter each other only occasionally, there is no particular need for them to think intensively about each other's feelings. But three people isolated in an enforced intimacy much closer than that of cellmates have to take thought. When one of them is responsible for the other two, tact has to be practiced painstakingly. When one of the three is a young man who doesn't believe that anything can happen to him because nothing ever has, the situation calls for extreme care. McCauley had to use his brains if Randy and Sammy Breen were to be able to work with him under exacting conditions like these.

He unhooked his space rope, rehooked it past a junction, and pulled himself toward the place where Sammy Breen had come to a stop. It was, of course, at a place where two of the frame pieces of the Platform should join a third. They were to be bolted together and then another long section of framework would be added, which in turn would have yet another beam placed and bolted to it so the construction could continue. At the moment, however, a bolt hole needed to be reamed so the parts could be bolted together.

McCauley arrived at the corner of a triangle. When linked to all the others, this triangle would ultimately support the skin and hold the interior partitions of the Platform. Again he slipped his space rope over the junction, hooked it, followed it, and went on toward the place where Sammy Breen was. Sammy's voice came out of his helmet phones.

"I saw a man do this once in a circus," said Sammy. "I thought he was wonderful. But I can do it!"

McCauley looked up. Sammy Breen had his space rope hooked around the girder, to be sure. But now he floated, head toward Earth, with one finger barely touching the metal beam. A photograph would have shown him apparently supporting his whole weight on a single finger. But here there was no weight. Nothing drew Sammy toward either Earth or the Platform. But for his space rope, the lightest thrust of his finger would have sent him floating slowly, implacably, helplessly away from the spidery floating object, to drift alone through space forever.

"I hope you checked your rope before you came outside," McCauley said dryly.

"I did," said Sammy nonchalantly. "It's okay."

He tried to pull himself back to the girder with his fingers. He couldn't quite reach it. He was no more than half an inch from a fingertip hold that would have been more than enough, but he couldn't make it. He reached and reached, and his movements made his body in its space suit revolve ridiculously upside down and otherwise. Then he couldn't get his hand anywhere near the girder.

McCauley watched. He was unreasonably tense. But Sammy rather sheepishly gave a tug on his space rope and floated back to firm contact with the Platform.

"Not to be finicky about it," said McCauley, "that wasn't wise. There was only one chance in ten thousand that anything could happen, but there was no need to take it."

"Yes, sir," said Sammy Breen.

McCauley settled down, three feet from the end of the beam that was to be bolted to the one that needed reaming. Sammy Breen gripped that beam between his thighs and hauled the reamer to his hand. At work on the Platform, in emptiness, a man did not carry things, he towed them on cords. If he let go of any untethered object it might stay where he put it, in mid-space, but it was much more likely to have some small motion relative to his which would make it drift placidly out of reach forever.

Sammy Breen set the reamer in place in the bolt hole and pulled its trigger. It cut metal. But it dragged unreasonably at him, trying to turn him in the direction opposite its own rotation. Tiny chips and metal dust twinkled in the fierce sunshine. They floated away. They would never fall to Earth. Never. The reamer went through and Sammy cut off its power. He tried to pull it out. It stuck.

McCauley watched. He'd made a rule that nobody should do anything in the least out of routine without another man nearby. The three of them did not work together at one spot ordinarily. In the kind of conditions customary here, they'd be hopelessly in each other's way. But he'd issued the order requiring two to be together on any unusual job. Now, having obeyed his own rule that there must be a second man at hand when anything beyond simple bolting was to be done, tact made him keep silent while Sammy did it his own way. Too-close supervision and too-constant instruction can make for inefficiency. Worse, on a job like building the

Platform, they can make for friction. McCauley watched without comment. He'd have done this thing differently. But it would be unwise to insist that it be done his way.

Sammy jerked at the reamer, which meant that he also jerked himself at it. He slid along the girder he gripped. McCauley said nothing. He'd criticized Sammy's horse-play a moment earlier. He did not want to make a second criticism now.

Sammy reached out—it would not be true to say that he stood up—and put his foot beside the reamer in the bolt hole. The position gave him leverage. He pulled violently. It was a wholly reasonable, completely natural, thoroughly matter-of-fact action. A man pulling something stuck in a hole braces himself exactly that way to get a strong pull at it. But this was on the Space Platform, where there is no weight.

The reamer gave. It came out abruptly. Sammy Breen shot away from the beam to the full length of his space rope—and the space rope slid off the end of the beam. He was headed for infinity with the reamer in his hand.

McCauley grabbed. He never knew how he managed to make so swift a motion in his clumsy space suit. But he hurled his body forward and snatched at the same instant. He caught the rope. But to reach it he'd had to lose his own leg-grip on the beam. The impetus of Sammy's leap jerked savagely at him. He squeezed his legs together in a frantic effort to hold fast by friction. He tried to turn his toes in to catch hold before he slid completely clear. But the feet of space suits do not pivot laterally so he could not turn them inward. Holding fast to Sammy's space rope, he was jerked inexorably clear and he and Sammy Breen floated away to emptiness together.

It was neither a rapid motion nor a simple one. The jerk had come at an angle rather than straight out. The two of them revolved slowly around each other at the two ends of the rope. McCauley held on grimly, braced for the countervailing tug of his own rope when it tightened.

It did tighten. And then it slid. The spot where Sammy had meant to bolt two girders together was, naturally, the point where the two frame members would complete a new triangle. It was to form one of the triangular facets of the twenty-sided figure the Platform would constitute when completed. But....

McCauley's rope slid, and caught, and slid again. Then it came free. Before it came free it had slowed the two of them, to be sure. It increased the rate of their spin. But it slid off to emptiness and the two of them went away from the Platform, revolving fairly rapidly about each other, held together by Sammy's space rope.

Their speed around each other was greater than the speed at which, as a pair, they were drifting serenely away. At one point in each rotation one of them approached the Platform while the other moved away from it. A second later the other spun toward the Platform and the first one moved toward emptiness. But together they drifted very, very deliberately toward the stars.

McCauley swore. Then he said curtly:

"Lieutenant!" The use of the term instead of the name was wise. Sammy Breen might be a horrified young man. But Lieutenant Breen was something else.

"Sir," said his voice unsteadily in McCauley's headphones, "I'm sorry, sir. I should have...."

"I'm going to throw you my space rope," snapped McCauley. "You will catch it and obey my orders."

"Yes, sir."

"Catch!" snapped McCauley.

He threw the rope. Because they were rotating, the first cast was wild. Sammy Breen wasn't where he threw the rope when it got to him. It had McCauley's own speed of rotation, so it did not go where he aimed. It took half a dozen attempts to get the rope to where the younger man could catch the squirming line in the stiff gauntlet of his space suit.

"Now, fasten your reamer to the rope," commanded McCauley. "Tie on your other tools. Give me every bit of equipment you've got except your air tanks."

"Y-yes, sir," said Sammy's voice in the helmet phones.

Spinning as they were, the universe of stars and sun and the vast, unfamiliar, brilliantly lighted object which was Earth seemed to be engaged in a monstrous saraband. Now Sammy was a glaringly bright object with full, blazing sunshine hitting his space suit. Again he was lighted from the side with the brightness of Earth behind him, racing past his body with all its features blurred. Yet again the stars seemed not points of light but streaks, and there were moments when the sun itself was a flashing band of intolerable brightness. But somehow this vast and silent motion of the cosmos seemed unreal. It was like a hallucination. It was like a nightmare in which absolutely nothing was true; in which there was no actual sun or Earth or stars, because in reality those things did not swing in lunatic sweeps around anybody, anywhere.

While the younger man blindly obeyed McCauley, they continued to drift away toward infinity. Curiously enough, the centrifugal force caused by their spinning gave McCauley the only sensation of weight that he'd had since his arrival at the orbit of the Platform.

Randy's voice came in McCauley's headphones.

"Ed! My God!"

His tone was anguished and hopeless.

"Randy," said McCauley in clipped tones. "You can be useful. When we're in line with you, say 'tip.' Say it again. Keep it up."

Almost instantly Randy said, "Tip." Then, "Tip." Then, "Tip" again. Sammy Breen said hoarsely:

"All my equipment, sir, is fastened to your space rope. Everything but my air tanks."

"Right. Now let go of it," commanded McCauley. "Randy, how fast are we drifting away?"

Randy's voice came hoarse and harsh.

"I don't know. Slowly, but you're a good hundred and fifty feet off. A trifle more."

McCauley calculated aloud, for his own comfort as well as the information of Randy and Sammy Breen.

"We've been drifting maybe half a minute. Those 'tips' of yours were about one second apart. We're spinning once in two seconds at the ends of a thirty-foot rope. Each of us has an angular velocity of something over forty feet per second. Forty-five or better. Our joint speed away from the Platform—a hundred and fifty feet in thirty seconds.... Somewhere around five feet per second. Not much more, anyhow! We're practically crawling away, but we're spinning like blazes."

Randy said, dry-throated:

"Even if we had rope, Ed, I couldn't get it to you."

"I know," said McCauley curtly. "Lieutenant?"

"Yes, sir," said Sammy Breen's voice, quite steady now. "I've thought of something, sir. If we act fast and I cut the rope at just the right instant, sir...."

"Keep quiet!" snapped McCauley. "That's an order! Right now I want you to push that equipment at the end of my rope away from you as hard as you can, in the direction we're spinning. The way we're spinning! You've got too much angular velocity. Understand?"

"Yes, sir," said Sammy. "I'm glad, sir...."

"Keep quiet!" snapped McCauley again. "Push!"

The cumbersome and weighty mass of equipment, which on Earth would have weighed nearly as much as Sammy Breen, swung away from him. It went around until it was behind McCauley. There was now a system of three weights on a string. The middle one, which was McCauley, did not spin around. He only rotated. The others swung in a wide circle about him.

"Get set, Randy," he said sharply, "and have your rope ready."

"What...." Then Randy understood. He swore.

McCauley let go of Sammy Breen's space rope at an instant when in his circle around McCauley he moved toward the Platform. At that instant, of course, McCauley still moved away. But he let go. The result was that he sent Sammy Breen floating back toward the spidery metal framework, and he himself moved away faster. In effect, he'd taken to himself a large part of Sammy's momentum toward destruction. But not quite all. There was still Sammy's equipment, which formed a new two-weight system of masses spinning about a common center of gravity. Yet it did look as if he'd seen the possibility of saving one of the two of them, and had taken the action which gave that chance at life to Lieutenant Sammy Breen.

"Major!" Sammy cried out desperately. "This is all wrong! It was my fault! I should have cut the rope! I protest, sir...."

"Shut up!" rasped McCauley. "Within a minute or two you'll float to the Platform. It's not likely you'll strike a beam direct. Get ready to throw your rope to Captain Hall so he can pull you in!"

Now he cut his own space rope and held its end. With Sammy Breen gone away toward life, he and the mass of equipment at the rope's other end still had a spinning motion. But it was a slow one. Yet he could repeat the same trick he'd worked with Sammy, though not with the same effectiveness. He could sacrifice the weight at the end of his rope, just as before he'd sacrificed himself. If he chose the moment when in their spinning the heavy objects were moving fastest toward the stars, that would be the moment when his own motion toward annihilation was least.

He let go. The awkward clump of tethered space equipment went swiftly toward nowhere. McCauley seemed to cease to drift away from where Sammy Breen, floating steadily, made bubbling noises to himself as if he were sobbing in shame that McCauley had given him life at the expense of his own. McCauley was now a good six hundred feet off in emptiness from the lacework of silvery bars.

"How am I doing, Randy?" asked McCauley curtly. "You want to catch Sammy when he comes through the framework. Get to where you can help him. But when you have time, make an estimate on me."

There was silence. The Platform hurtled on around Earth. The changing, distorted patterns of land and sea seemed to writhe as they went past in the intolerably brilliant sunshine. But over at the very edge of the bright disk a little trace of blackness appeared. That would be the night line on Earth. The Platform and its company moved separately yet together toward that darkness. Presently it would cover half the disk of Earth, and then it would sweep on until only a swiftly thinning crescent of light remained, and then the Platform would plunge into utter darkness, where most of the cosmos was only shining stars and a pallid moon, the rest the blackness of the Pit. And of course, in this darkness the building satellite's unprotected substance would—like McCauley— drop to a temperature of two hundred and twenty-odd degrees below zero.

"Throw your rope to Captain Hall!" McCauley snapped to Sammy Breen. "I know you'll turn somersaults. But throw it!"

Silence again. McCauley made his own estimate. It was not good. He did not drift swiftly away into the emptiness which would presently be blackness and cold and death. But he had not lost all his velocity away from the Platform.

He took the wrench with which he fastened together the frame members of the unlikely object which he left with such deadly deliberation. He drew up his feet below him. He placed the wrench under them. At a carefully chosen instant he thrust it violently away.

He pushed the wrench toward nothingness. Its mass may have been ten pounds on Earth. His own mass, with his space suit and air tanks and the like, was probably thirty times as much. If he thrust the wrench away at thirty feet per second—and he did—he would change his own velocity by one foot per second. This might mean a slowing of his motion away, or it might mean a terribly slow drift back to the Platform and a chance for life.

He took his space knife. It might weigh a pound. He threw it. Systematically and unhurriedly he denuded his belt of the tools hanging to it. A mass of possibly sixty pounds, thrown violently away, changed his velocity by as much as six or—considering that he had less mass with each bit of mass he discarded—probably seven feet per second.

"I've got Sammy," said Randy's voice, hoarse and strained. "He's all right.... You don't seem to be going away any more, Ed. You're no farther than you were. Maybe I can knot ropes.... No. There aren't enough."

"Right," said McCauley with an odd calm. "There wouldn't be time, anyhow. We're heading for eclipse. I've got to get back on my own—and fast. The storybooks say rockets are used by men in space to go bobbing around in their space suits. We know better. But I'm going to use one air tank."

He writhed in the harness outside his space suit. He managed to detach one of his two air tanks. He aimed its pipe carefully.

Air poured out with a rush when he opened the stop-cock. There was two thousand pounds pressure to begin with. The tank had been in unshielded sunshine for more than an hour. The effective pressure of the air had tripled, at least, because of its rise in temperature. It made a rocket jet of gas. McCauley could feel its quick, sharp tug at him.

It went empty.

He put it under his feet and gave it the most violent of thrusts toward the Milky Way. Now he could see that he had given the discarded things all the momentum that had carried him away from the Platform, plus all he had taken from Sammy Breen. He was moving toward the Platform. It no longer dwindled as time went by. It grew in size with an intolerable, incredible slowness. But that slowness amounted to doom.

"You're headed back," said Randy's agonized voice in his helmet phones. "But it's slow, Ed! It's desperately slow!"

The blackness, which was Earth's own shadow cast upon its night-side surface, was now fully halfway from the rim of the world toward that halfway point which was the middle of the space that Earth occupied within the cosmos.

"There's about fifteen minutes left before totality," said McCauley with deliberation. "I've one more thing I can throw away. But I need to steer with it too, and I can't be accurate at this distance. I don't dare to use it from so far away. I've no space rope left to throw for you to catch. I have to throw that last thing away at the very last instant."

He heard confused sounds. Sammy Breen, back at the Platform, made incoherent noises. He probably gesticulated, because Randy understood.

"Yes," said Randy's voice harshly. "Make it quick. But take care! More than your own life depends on your being careful now!"

Sammy Breen gulped. McCauley heard him. Then silence again.

It was necessary to wait. McCauley was a tiny, glistening object in emptiness, a desperately long way from the equally glistening Platform. He turned slowly, foolishly, as he floated. Away off against a background of stars—but the sun moved momentarily nearer its edge—there was a shape that now was not quite half of a circle of brilliant light, and more than half of a circle of darkness like that of the Abyss. It did not look like Earth. It had not the least appearance of a world in which human beings lived and moved and breathed and loved and died. It was a monstrosity whose details changed their shape as half minutes and quarter minutes went by. And continually and implacably the darkness spread over more of it.

Randy's voice came desperately.

"Hurry, Sammy! Give it to me and get back into the cabin. We won't have time to wait our turns at the air lock.... Right! Now get back in the cabin!"

"How am I doing now, Randy?" McCauley asked calmly. "How's my line of motion?"

"I don't like it!" said Randy fiercely. "It's off to one side! Sammy just brought me all the extra space ropes. He tied them together inside. I'm checking them now. There are four of them."

McCauley said:

"I hate to seem overanxious, but how much will I miss the Platform by?"

"Too much," answered Randy bitterly. "What have you got left that you can throw away to steer by?"

"Eighty pounds of mass," said McCauley with composure. "But I have to wait until the last second."

Silence again. Darkness covered three-quarters of the Earth's strange disk. It was not the darkness of a night on Earth, with trees and plants and men as darker shapes against starlit or moonlit ground or sea. It was the blackness of nothingness, of annihilation.

"You can't stay out much longer, Randy," McCauley said. "I'll have to try it."

"There's the moon," said Randy hoarsely. "I can see by that, ... maybe."

Again silence. The shape which was Earth became the thinnest of crescents. The sun blazed fiercely almost at its outer rim.

The sun turned orange, crimson, ruby-red. It ceased to be a circle. One edge blacked out. It was half blacked out. It was gone.

McCauley wriggled in the harness outside his space suit. He spoke deliberately.

"I'm going to take all the deep breaths I can, Randy. I'll even let a little extra pressure into my suit. Then I'll take off my last air tank and try to steady myself with its jet of air. Then I'll put it under my feet and jump against it, toward you. Now listen! If anything goes wrong, it won't be your fault! Understand? Don't take any crazy risks. If I go on past the Platform, get into the cabin fast before the cold comes! That is my order! I expect you to obey it!"

"Cripes, Ed!" Randy's voice broke.

McCauley bled air into his suit. He breathed deeply and fast, saturating his lungs with oxygen. He removed the tank and then spent precious seconds stripping away the harness that had held tools and extra equipment to his suit.

He jetted away the air. In the utter silence that was the universe, the whistle of escaping compression was conducted to his gloved hands and so to the remaining air inside his space suit. He used the jet with infinite care. The tank tugged briefly and his random body rotation stopped. He saw the Platform, almost incredibly dim in the moonlight.

He jumped against the mass of the air tank and harness together. In seconds he could see that he was moving closer toward the silvery, spidery framework in the moonshine. He kept himself still. Nothing he could do now would add anything to his chance for life, and exertion would lessen the time left before he suffocated for lack of air.

He relaxed by an iron effort of will. He had gambled. He could win or he could lose. But he must keep the calmness of a man who sees the stakes down and waits for the outcome.

The Platform was no more than a hundred and fifty yards away. No more than a hundred.

He would miss it. He would pass sixty feet or more beyond its outermost edge. Randy would undoubtedly try to throw him the space ropes he'd tied together. The odds were enormously against his being able to catch them.

He said nothing. If Randy thought that he'd run out of air before he reached the point nearest the Platform, he would reproach himself less; he'd believe he couldn't have done anything, anyhow.

Fifty yards. Twenty. He saw glittering metal only sixty feet away. But there was no conceivable action he could take to move himself that sixty feet.

Then something dark came toward him. It grew larger. It was Randy, plunging out from the girders with a hundred and twenty feet of space rope trailing behind him, made fast to a firmly bolted beam.

He collided with McCauley. McCauley felt him gripping fiercely. He felt Randy clinging to him savagely against the jerk of the rope which must tighten presently.

The jerk came, violent and abrupt.

Randy gasped in relief. He took away one space-suited arm to haul at the space rope that had checked McCauley's slow drift past to nothingness.

"Very nice work, Randy," said McCauley composedly, "but you took an awful chance."

They bumped against the substance of the Platform—one square metal tube some three inches by five.

"Can you hold on?" demanded Randy, panting. "I'll give you one of my air tanks!"

They were out at the farthermost limit of the framework of the Space Platform. McCauley's faceplate began to frost now, with the loss of heat to the darkness.

"Make it fast," said McCauley. "We want to get in out of the cold."

Fumblings. Clatterings. McCauley heard Randy's teeth chatter, which might be cold or might be reaction from the terror he'd felt on McCauley's account.

"Right!" McCauley said suddenly. He felt air blowing past his face. Randy's extra tank was connected. "I'm all set now. Let's get headed for the cabin."

"Hold it!" said Randy angrily. "You tie a space rope to yourself and loop it around a beam! Do you want to take a chance on slipping away? Maybe there is only one chance in ten thousand of getting lost, but there's no need to take that!"

"Okay, boss," said McCauley. "I shoulda known better."

Hardly more than seconds later he was sliding toward the cabin, Randy following close behind. He came to a joint where three of the beams came together. He unlooped his space rope from the near side, looped it around beyond the joint, crawled over, and slid again.

The cold came fast, but they would make it. Already his mind was at work on a matter that bothered him. He was in charge of the building of the Platform. That meant that he had to think about the feelings of the men under him. Randy was all right. He'd done a good job, and he knew it. But Sammy Breen was different. He was a very young officer, and he felt right now that he'd blundered and imperiled a senior officer—practically killed him, in fact—and he'd be in a state of almost hysterical self-abasement. Not a good state for young officers to be in.

When McCauley squirmed out of the air lock, young Sammy Breen looked at him. He was deathly white and utterly ashamed.

"Hm," said McCauley ruefully. "Sammy, I think I'll have to report myself for incompetence. When a second man's standing by while somebody does a tricky job, he ought to be sure that his space rope can't slip. I didn't. I doggone near got you killed, Sammy. I'm sorry."

Sammy Breen made an inarticulate sound. Then Randy came out of the air lock.

"For the love of Heaven, Sammy!" he said, scolding. "It's your trick to fix food! We've got less than an hour for eating before the sun comes back. And you haven't even got the stuff heating up! What kind of a cook are you, anyhow?"

Sammy swallowed. He swallowed again. Neither McCauley nor Randy mentioned the late so nearly complete disaster. Randy was kidding him. McCauley made a joke of it, too.

Sammy put the food on to thaw and heat. He struggled to become worthy of the companionship of men like McCauley and Randy Hall. Presently he swallowed and said accusingly:

"You characters were late for dinner. Don't blame me if it's cold!"

He looked anxiously at them. He hoped....

McCauley grinned at him. Randy laughed. They laughed together. Lieutenant Sammy Breen felt wonderfully good. And he would be very careful hereafter.

4

(There was high adventure on the moon when it was first colonized. Men faced various ways of dying—all of them unpleasant—and found that simply staying alive was a great satisfaction and a full-time occupation. Because of this spirit— which is that of true adventure—there came to be bases where hydroponic gardens freshened the air and men took continued living as a matter of course. This, obviously, was not adventure. So problems arose. Men began to be moved by other motives than the zest they'd known at first. But there were still a great many ways of getting killed on the moon. So there came a time when Colonel Ed McCauley had to insist that certain men under his command put first things first, as adventurers do, and not act for the gratification of their problem personalities.)

***

Traveling at moon gait, which is the standard travel pace on Earth's big moon, McCauley had ten of the last twenty miles behind him when he saw the sledge trail in the dust. He frowned at it and looked over to the west. He saw Earth, blue-green and glamorous, hanging as usual in the lunar sky just above the edges of the ring mountains. But Earth was always just there. He squinted at the sun through the faceplate of his helmet. It was a trifle over ten degrees above the horizon and it moved across the black, star-speckled sky at half a degree per hour. In twenty hours, then, lunar night would fall. And here was the sledge track that said that the relay unit for Repeater Two, carrying word to and from Farside and the rest of the human race, had passed this way en route to be set up; but the lack of returning footprints said that the men with it had not come back.

Repeater One was already in place and ready to operate. Repeaters Three and Four had also been put in position by men from faraway Farside Base. Repeater Two was necessary to bring

Farside Base into communication with the rest of the cosmos. Two weeks of lunar night with no word from outside the base and not even Earth to look at in the sky—this would not be good for the men on Farside.

McCauley stopped. He'd been moving in that swooping, semi-flying fashion which the lesser lunar gravity allows. He stared at the trail. No, the men had not come back. Yet he'd ordered a party of two to set up the relay unit. It was to be put into place on the very tip of a mountain that was now away below the horizon. There it would be in line of sight of Repeater One, which was relatively near, and Repeater Three, which was farther away but which in turn could relay signals to Four, which was farthest away of all. From Four, the relayed messages would go on to Farside Base. When all this was accomplished, the Grimaldi Base ten miles distant could communicate with Farside through Repeaters One, Two, Three, and Four, and with Earth by line-of-sight transmission; so Farside could communicate with Earth and through Earth Relay with all the other moon bases—in short, with all humanity. But Two should have been up and in operation by now.

McCauley shook his head impatiently inside his space helmet. He'd been away from his command for thirty hours, during which he'd traveled twenty miles on foot, at moon gait, to Gerritson Bay. It wasn't a bay, of course, but an intrusion of now-frozen lava into the mountainous country here at the edge of the moon's earthside surface. He'd been met by a moon jeep and had traveled seven hundred miles over a mare—one of the dark areas that were once thought to be seas but actually were dry and level—to the main lunar base near Hipparchus. He'd had a one-hour conference with the base commander there, trying to work out something to prevent the first murder on Earth's big satellite. The conference was unsatisfactory. He'd come back to Gerritson Bay and now he'd covered ten of the twenty remaining miles to Grimaldi Base. When he reached Grimaldi the excessively irritating problem of a murder in the making was still unsolved, and now in addition there was the failure to complete placing the relay at the site of Repeater Two. The sledge ought to be in its place on the peak which was invisible from here, and the men who'd set it up should have returned. They hadn't.

He flipped on his space radio and said curtly:

"McCauley calling relay placing party. Come in!"

There was no answer. He called again and again. Then he called Grimaldi Base. Again no answer. He was out of radio contact with all humanity on the moon—even his own base ten miles away—though by switching frequencies he could raise Earth Relay a quarter million miles farther away. The men with the moon sledge might only be behind a mountain wall or anywhere in any direction below the horizon, but radio communication on the moon is limited to line-of-sight because there is no air and hence no layer of ions to bounce radio signals down behind obstacles or around the moon's curvature.

McCauley started off again, fuming. Moon gait is a highly specialized form of travel. In one-sixth gravity a man can cover ten miles an hour over rough ground if he knows the trick of the gait and the trail is marked. He travels in slow-motion giant steps, with something of the effect of an extremely deliberate ballet. He begins with a leap up and forward, and he rises slowly and deliberately while soaring ahead. At mid-leap he is six feet higher than at take-off. Then he descends slowly and with dignity, touches ground and strides at the same time, and bounds up and ahead once more. There are long seconds between steps and long yards between strides. When a person is used to it, moon gait is almost restful. Some people even find it familiar. They've dreamed of such effortless half flight in their sleep.

Now, though he was disturbed, McCauley made two miles with no other known cause for worry than the lateness of the two men who'd placed the relay and the prospective killing he'd had on his mind before. He passed between precipices and over dust-strewn stone and through winding defiles. The two men should be back....

Then he spotted something. Abruptly he raised his arms and extended both feet before him. He came down to the ground and stopped short. Then—not soaring this time—he walked back to an object on the trail.

It was an air tank, exactly like the two tanks at the back of his own space suit. It had been dropped from the moon sledge. It would hold air for one man for three hours.

Men driving a moon sledge would wear one tank on their space suits for safety, and they'd shed one for lightness. They'd breathe from the much larger tanks on the sledge itself while they traveled. Spare and extra tanks like this would ride on the sledge. It was not easy to imagine that it had dropped. One man would go on ahead of the sledge and one would follow. It was hard to believe that the second man would not notice the loss of an air tank. Air tanks were life. True, a sledge party always had more air than was needed for any expected journey—a good margin for emergency—but this tank could cut the margin for this journey seriously.

McCauley growled to himself. He knew the calculations for placing the relay. The mountain beyond the horizon was an eight-hour journey by sledge—the horizon on the moon is only two miles away instead of eight. Breathing from the sledge, the men would arrive with one tank on their suits untapped, another, also untapped, to be mounted; and an extra tank for good measure. When they'd put the sledge in place and aired its beams and set up the nondirectional auxiliary antennae, they'd start back with two full tanks each and another one for reserve. They'd make better time coming back—six hours, no more. And each man had a full six hours on his back, and there were three additional hours in the extra they'd take turns carrying. It was ample margin. But now the spare tank was left behind. There was no margin.

McCauley tried to lift the tank. But it had lain in the shadow of a boulder, out of the sun's fierce glare—on moon dust, radiating heat away toward the stars. It had cooled off to the temperature of a shadow, two hundred and forty degrees below zero. It was frozen. The air was liquid air. The tank was more brittle than glass was.

It slipped, striking the boulder. It cracked and broke. A glistening liquid poured out and evaporated instantly. Where it fell into shadow, part of it froze and then vanished more quickly than any earthly frost.

McCauley growled again. Air was precious on the moon. But

there was no use crying when it was spilt. He turned around and began his journey again. He had good reason to worry now.

He was a singular, slow-motion soaring figure in a polished silvery space suit. Where there was a rise in the ground, he came smoothly up from behind it, the glaring sun glowing on his space armor. Extending one leg in what might pass as a version of a choreographer's arabesque, he came down on the extended foot and stepped on it, floating gently upward and forward swiftly in a continued series of seeming flights. He went through winding passes where the sledge trail was plain in the dust below him, he soared across preposterous areas strewn with boulders the size of apartment houses. Once, going through a narrow gap in the wall of an unnamed crater—a very small one, barely two miles across—he passed a spot which showed that the two men had changed places. The one in advance had gone to the rear, and the one who'd been behind now led the way.

It was just beyond the farther wall of the crater that he saw the second air tank, dropped in the trail.

It could not possibly be an accident. A moon sledge has racks for carrying air tanks. It was conceivable that a tank could have slid out and been lost unnoticed. But it was starkly inconceivable that it could have happened twice.

McCauley raged suddenly. He knew what had happened, he knew why it had happened, he knew who was involved. He flipped the base-frequency switch.

"Holmes! Kent! Come in!" he snapped. "Grimaldi Base, come in! Holmes! Kent! Come in! Grimaldi Base, come in!"

He did not try to pick up the second air tank. Instead, he increased his speed over the fantastic landscape of riven stone and upthrust rock. He went faster, floating twenty and thirty yards at a bound and calling angrily into the eternal silence about him. This higher speed was not particularly safe. A stumble on any of his landings could have meant a nasty crash and possibly a smashed helmet plate. But he raged on. He'd just traveled nearly a quarter of the way around the moon to try to effect the quiet and nonspectacular prevention of a murder. Now he found his trouble wasted, his precautions nullified, and the operation of his base imperiled. Moreover, the welfare of the men on Farside was threatened drastically. They might have to go through an entire lunar night, two weeks long, without any contact with other human beings.

Long, long minutes of speeded-up moon gait went by, the suit radio sending out snapped calls for Holmes and Kent to answer or, failing them, for Grimaldi Base to reply.

He was less than five miles from the base when he got an answer to his call. He'd climbed gradually to a high plateau which now dropped downward again so that what seemed an infinity of explosion-scarred desolation lay before him. He was in line of sight of Grimaldi.

"Grimaldi answers," said a voice in his helmet phones. "Grimaldi answers. Over."

Words fairly burst from McCauley's lips, though the rhythm of his twenty- and thirty-yard leaps remained unbroken.

"How in the blistering Gehenna," he rasped, "did Holmes and Kent get out of the base together? What fool sent them off?"

The voice in his headphones jerked a little.

"Why—it was your order, sir! A relay from Earth came in. Holmes was on monitor duty. He wrote down the order, sir. You ordered him and Kent to take the sledge with the relay unit for Repeater Two and set it up where it belonged, sir."

McCauley almost strangled in his wrath.

"Have they got there yet?"

"No, sir. They should use it to report that it's operating, sir. They haven't."

"When they do," rasped McCauley, "tell them that I specifically order them to stay in communication with you until I get there! Absolutely no excuse will be accepted for failure! I'm less than five miles off. I should get there in a quarter of an hour—twenty minutes at the outside. They think they're smart, but they've slipped up this time! Tell them that!"

"Y-yes, sir."

The headphone clicked.

McCauley uttered some profane words in the close confines of his space helmet. Back at Lunar Base he'd laid the matter of Holmes and Kent before the commanding officer, who was the ranking officer on the moon. Kent was an able young officer, transferred to Space Service from the Air Force. Holmes was also an able young officer, who'd been a submariner before he transferred to the equally confining Space Service. They'd known each other back on Earth and somehow—nobody knew how—a bitter and inveterate enmity had sprung up between them. Perhaps a girl was at the root of it, but if so, neither of them won her. Perhaps, by this time, the initial cause of their hatred had nearly or completely ceased to matter. Enmity does not often last unless things occur that can feed and strengthen it. It is normal for two young men to quarrel furiously and be ready to kill each other. But if they are separated long enough, their hatred usually dies away to acute dislike. In time the dislike fades to mere aversion or they may forget their anger altogether. But this happens when there is nothing to sustain and increase the quarrel.

On the other hand, if they come across each other often enough, and more especially if they try to harm each other, what could have begun as mere indignation and contempt can build up into a blind and murderous fury at the mere sight or thought of each other. How it started does not matter then. McCauley suspected that this was the case with Kent and Holmes.

Swinging up and soaring ahead, touching ground with precision at each landing and swinging up again to strange, wingless flight, McCauley muttered to himself.

They'd been assigned to his command. Not knowing—then— he'd introduced them. They spoke with great politeness but did not shake hands. Settling down to the routine and tedium of a six-man base, it became evident that there was something wrong. There was no overt trouble, but there was strain. It showed in a thousand trivial ways. When a party went out on an errand which required traveling for days in roasting sunlight, cased in space suits that were almost as confining as strait jackets, under conditions which rasped the nerves and tried the tempers of everybody, Holmes and Kent very nearly caused disasters.

Hatred blazed between them. When their records arrived at Grimaldi Base, McCauley realized that the beginning of this hatred could not matter any more. They'd hated each other so long and so bitterly that if they were asked the reason they'd have panted about something done yesterday or last month or last year—and perhaps never have gotten back to the beginning. They might even have forgotten it. But there was a strangeness in their enmity. They did not simply want disaster and misfortune to befall each other. They hungered to be disaster, they thirsted to be misfortune, each for the other. And somehow there was a demoniac pride involved. In the days of the duello there would have been a simple and normal solution. They would have met in stately fashion with swords or pistols, and they would have fought to the death under the eyes of seconds and witnesses, and somehow it would have been appropriate.

But such things were impossible now. The code of the duello was outmoded. So when McCauley read the records and reports on the two men—because a commanding officer needs to know the men who serve under him, and the more dangerous the service the better he needs to know them—he knew that the first case of murder on the moon was in the making. Since they couldn't fight formally, as in olden times, what must happen would amount to murder.

There'd been an automobile accident at Earth Base of the Space Service. It looked very much as if it were deliberate, as if Holmes and Kent had contrived it by agreement between themselves so that one was bound to be killed. Both were hurt. Neither died. Then there was the time when Kent was found with a rifle in his hand and a bullet wound in his shoulder, ignoring the wound and passionately pursuing a hunt for—so he said—a deer. He explained that the wound was an accident. The records showed that Holmes was hunting in the same area at the same time. They showed that he had a slight flesh wound—made by a bullet. Both Holmes and Kent gave totally unconvincing accounts of their wounds, and each denied that he had been wounded by the other. Their stories did not satisfy their commanding officer. He transferred them to other units, and in his confidential comment on their records—comment they would never see—he said that he believed they'd arranged a duel in deer-hunting country with big-game rifles, contrived so the one who was killed would seem to be the victim of a hunting accident. It could not be proved, but he believed it.

There were other memos. Neither Holmes nor Kent had a mark against him except in connection with the other man. Yet no commanding officer—certainly none on the moon—would want either man in his base after having read the records. The moon is too small for men who carry their enmities with them into space.

And McCauley had both men—able men, capable men, desirable men except for their mutual hatred. He'd traveled a quarter way around the moon to have one or both of them transferred out of Grimaldi Base before they could arrange another covered-up duel which would leave one dead and the other a murderer. But his effort had been futile. They couldn't be transferred out immediately. They couldn't be gotten out, for it was too close to sunset. They couldn't be gotten away at all during the lunar night. And now they were out on Farside where there could be no witnesses and the grave of a murdered man could never be found.

McCauley arrived, raging mad, at the small, grubby, dust-insulated dome that was Grimaldi Base. No report had come in from Kent or Holmes. McCauley was bitterly sure that they'd gone out to the blasted moonscape firmly resolved that only one of them would return. Somehow, in the illimitable emptiness of which the fiftieth part had never been seen by men, somehow, under the black, star-studded sky with the setting sun casting mile-long shadows of utter blackness and absolute cold, McCauley knew that they would have some sort of fight in which one must die.

But they were Space Service officers. Before they had that fight they would set up the relay that would give Farside Base a connection to Grimaldi, and so to Earth, and so by Earth Relay to every other human being on the moon. They would do their duty as Space Service officers before they did murder.

Stooping, McCauley came out of the air lock into the base.

"I want all the facts about Kent and Holmes!" he snapped.

"No word from them yet, sir," said the communications officer. "But we've picked up clickings, sir, which might be the unit being put into operation. But Holmes and Kent have two beams to align, sir, besides the all-direction antennae. They may be checking with Farside, sir, to make sure the relay beam is pointed right to that base."

McCauley stripped off his space suit.

"They're in more trouble than they know," he growled. "They lost two air tanks off their sledge."

The communications officer's mouth dropped open.

"But Colonel, sir.... They couldn't! They need those tanks to get back with!"

"Exactly," McCauley snapped. "Route the relay's local-antenna and suit-radio frequencies in to me. I'll take the messages."

He stamped through the cramped and shabby little base to the minute compartment set aside for the Base Commander's office. It was approximately four feet by six. He settled down in the one chair, glowering. Automatically he glanced at the dials that reported conditions at the base. Outside temperature facing sun, 198°. Shadow temperature, minus 205°. Inside barometric pressure, 30.02 inches. Inside temperature, 72°. Carbon monoxide, 28 parts per million. Carbon dioxide, 1.8%. Oxygen, 21.2%.

The physical state of the base was good. But there were two men out on Farside who lacked two tanks of air they needed to get back. Although it was their intention that only one of them should return, they'd outsmarted themselves. Neither could get back, now.

A clicking from a loud-speaker. A wavery voice:

"Calling Grimaldi Base! Calling Grimaldi! Call...."

"Calling Repeater Two," said McCauley. He was very grim. "Calling Repeater Two!"

"... rimaldi Ba...." Silence, then suddenly: "Hello!"

It was Holmes' voice. McCauley recognized it.

"Holmes!" he said curtly. "You two fools have committed suicide! You dropped one air tank off the sledge. Remember? That meant that only one of you could get back, and you and Kent could decide later which one it would be. But Kent kicked an air tank off, too! Now who's coming back?"

There was a startled silence.

"You heard me!" said McCauley savagely. "There were three tanks on that sledge. They'd bring you both back with air to spare.

But you threw one away, and Kent threw one away, and so there's one left. It's six hours' travel back to here, and you've air for two men for four and a half!"

Again silence. McCauley could envision the scene at Repeater Two, to which his voice was transmitted by precisely the system of beam relay used on Earth to carry telephone messages across continents without wires. There would be two bulky, space-suited figures atop an irregularly level space from which the ground fell away on every side, a drop of thousands of feet. They would be in glaring sunlight from the lowest of low-hanging suns. Where it struck the metal of their space armor they would glitter blindingly. Where there was shadow, there would be the blackness of the pit. Overhead there stretched a black sky with a thousand million stars, and around and below them there would be long, angular, parallel ribbons of shadow with sharply defined sides and with beginnings but no ends. And there would be the moon sledge with the relay built solidly upon it, its runners chocked with stony debris so it would not slide or topple. There would be the two bowl-shaped beam reflectors, one pointing back to Repeater One—itself a moon sledge wedged in place upon a mountain—and the other to remoteness and to wildness and to night.

"You could come back as you went," said McCauley. "You could bring back the sledge, breathing air from its tanks on the trip. But if you did that, Farside would be out of communication during the coming night. That would have to be explained."

Again it seemed that he could see the faraway, motionless figures of the two men listening over their suit radios to the voice twice relayed before it could reach their ears.

"I would have to explain," said McCauley grimly, "that Lieutenants Kent and Holmes intended to murder each other, and each one threw away an air tank he expected the other man to use—but he expected to have plenty of air for himself! I would have to explain that Farside was isolated because two would-be murderers had outsmarted themselves and didn't have the guts to face the consequences!"

Kent's voice came from a speaker. He spoke from that distant mountain peak toward which darkness crept steadily.

"Look here, sir." His tone was defiant.

"If that sledge is brought back," said McCauley angrily, "I'll court-martial whoever comes back with it, even the two of you! If one of you comes back, there'll be a court of inquiry. Maybe you've worked out a pretty story of an accident for the survivor to tell. But you can't use it now, because I found the air tanks you threw away! If one of you comes back, the inquiry will end in a court-martial and a murder verdict!"

Holmes' voice, stiff and steady, was as defiant as Kent's had been.

"I take it, sir, that you're advising neither of us to come back. Very well, sir! We've a little matter to settle between us. We can settle that and the one who's left...."

"If neither of you comes back," rasped McCauley, "the inquiry into your deaths will inform an interested world that two officers— and supposedly gentlemen—of the Space Service were actually two smart, snide, shabby killers who overreached themselves! The Service will be proud to have it known that its officers try to murder each other by throwing away each other's air tanks. The Service will be very, very proud!"

The irony of the last words was corrosive.

"Sir...." The two voices spoke together, outraged and despairing. "Sir," panted Kent's voice, alone. "We'd no idea of anything like that, sir! We've always hated each other, but...."

His voice ended in a gulp. McCauley growled. A young officer can be very much of a fool, of course, but he can be desperately solicitous for the honor of the Service to which he is attached. McCauley spoke with icy precision.

"I am not concerned with your lives or your hatreds or your intentions. I am concerned with the good name of the Space Service. I order you both to come back here. Alive. Together. You will start immediately!"

A dazed silence. Then Kent said:

"But—you don't want us to bring the sledge...."

"And we haven't—" this was Holmes—"we haven't enough air to get back! How can we do it, sir?"

McCauley relaxed in his small cubbyhole of an office. Very privately he drew a breath of relief. But his tone remained stern.

"You will head for Repeater One. If you remember, my voice goes from the base here to Repeater One where it is relayed to Repeater Two. If I chose the proper frequency it would go on through Three and Four to Farside. Can you think of any advantage in being at Repeater One instead of Two?"

A long pause. Then Holmes' voice, dubious:

"It's nearer the base, sir. No more than three hours' travel, if that much. We could make it on one tank of air apiece, sir, and have the extra one for margin. We could make it to base from there, sir, if we were there. But we're not, and it's three hours' travel from here! We'd get there...."

"You would get there?" demanded McCauley ominously. "Or you will get there?"

"Will, sir." But the young officer's voice was bewildered.

"For your information," said McCauley curtly, "the Repeater One relay unit is exactly like the relay unit at Repeater Two. I may add that it is in bright sunshine, but will not be so indefinitely."— This was because McCauley remembered an air tank which had lain in shadow until its metal shivered brittlely when struck and the air inside it was a liquid. "It was carried to its position and mounted exactly as the relay for Repeater Two was. Now figure it out for yourself! If you still don't understand when you get to it, call me from there. Now get moving! Sunset's not far away."

He clicked off his microphone, but left the receiving unit on. The relay at Repeater Two would pick up suit-radio speech and relay it back, the pickup being from its all-direction antennae. McCauley heard mumblings. Then, very distinctly, Holmes spoke.

"Understand, I'm going to cooperate with you, getting to Repeater One, but that doesn't mean I like you any better!"

Kent said resentfully:

"I figured you'd have to fight me for the air to get back with. And you pulled the same trick on me! But we'll manage eventually...."

More mutterings. Then:

"Cripes! Let's get going!"

There were those peculiar noises which a microphone inside a space suit picks up and transmits. Breathings. Clankings. Sometimes the squeak of metal sliding on metal.

McCauley listened. Presently the noises faded and ceased. The two young space-suited officers had descended the mountain to where they were not in line of sight of the relay, and consequently it could not pick up their suit-radio communications to relay back to McCauley.

The communications officer tapped on the office door.

"We're through to Farside Base, sir," he reported. "The relay system's working splendidly. Farside just asked for an Earth Relay link to Lunar Base."

"Give it to 'em," said McCauley succinctly.

He waited, listening. He had Repeater One as well as Two set so it would retransmit any local pickup on helmet-phone frequency, but it was half an hour before anything but the peculiar singing murmurs of empty space came from the loud-speaker. Then he heard heavy breathing.

He heard a colloquy between Kent and Holmes, far away in the lunar mountains. They were evidently climbing somewhere, and part of the climb necessarily took them through deep shadow, where the temperature of the rock was down to night temperature. Their space suits could handle the cold for a certain length of time, but the teeth of one of the men were chattering before he came out into sunlight at the end of the climb.

McCauley heard Holmes say sarcastically:

"I needed that last pull. Want me to thank you for it?"

Kent's voice snapped as he answered Holmes.

"I did it solely because McCauley would court-martial me if I came in alone!"

A pause, then the remote, transmitted sound of space shoes on stone. Holmes spoke.

"There's a way I can kill you easily. All I need do is get myself killed."

He laughed without mirth, and Kent said bitterly, "Go ahea—" Then there was silence.

The communications officer brought McCauley a message from

Lunar Base congratulating Grimaldi Base for completing the communications link between the two hemispheres of the moon.

"All right. Forget it," McCauley said.

He continued to listen. An hour went by. Then, without warning, there came an explosive "Look out!" There was a crash and then panting. Kent's voice rasped, "Have you gotten killed?" Holmes answered through clenched teeth. "Not yet. But how will I get out of here?" More clankings; more words, painstakingly devoid of solicitude on the one hand, or any amiable emotion such as gratitude on the other. McCauley could visualize exactly what was going on from the words. Holmes had fallen into a pothole, one of innumerable such mantraps scattered at random everywhere.

Kent got him out. Holmes grunted to indicate that he could do without more help. That was that. Minutes later, McCauley heard Kent say dourly:

"Three hours to Repeater One? We're over three hours now. How's your air?"

"All right," Holmes snapped. "When we get to that level place, we'll split the extra tank."

McCauley fretted. He could not know how far or how fast the two men were moving, off in that deadly waste of obstacles. Three hours had seemed a fair estimate. But plainly they'd had trouble.

Their voices cut off before they reached a spot where they could divide the air in the tank that had to be shared.

Then silence, for a long, long time. When McCauley heard any sound again, it was Holmes angrily calling to Kent, demanding that he say whether he needed help or not. And then for a full half hour McCauley listened to the sharp-voiced, sometimes abusive exchanges between the two. Kent had touched the keystone of an unstable rock slope. It gave way under him and went whirling downward in one of those infrequent, slow-motion moon avalanches that are unimaginable until one has seen them. Kent checked himself on the edge of a precipice over which the rolling stones fell in utter silence until after tens of seconds they struck and split, still noiselessly.

He could not get away. It was dangerous to help him, lest

another avalanche be started. McCauley, listening, sweated as he glanced at a clock. But Holmes was helping Kent.

Later—much later—he heard clatterings and Kent's voice said snappishly:

"Well, here's Repeater One. McCauley said to come here. What do we do now? I've air for fifteen minutes more."

Holmes tried to speak, but couldn't. There were clankings.

"Doggone you," Kent snarled shrilly, "you cheated on the air! You didn't split even! Cripes!"

Then he panted, and suddenly there was a hissing sound, and gasps. McCauley's hands were tightly clenched as the sounds came to him from both faraway space-suit microphones. But at the hissing sound he relaxed.

A little later Holmes' voice came, astonished.

"That was it! He said that the relay here was exactly like the relay at Repeater Two. It's a sledge, and it was brought here by two men—and it has air tanks that they breathed from while they traveled! Kent, you hooked me to the air. The pressure's way up! We can refill our suit tanks and the spare!"

Kent said waspishly:

"So I noticed. Get your tank full-up and let me have my share.... McCauley said to call him from here if we needed to. What say?"

"McCauley can go to blazes!" rumbled Holmes. "It's not two hours from here to the base. If we fill up on air, we can get there before sunset. To heck with McCauley!"

In the commanding officer's cubbyhole at Grimaldi Base, McCauley relaxed again in his chair. His expression went from strain to contentment. He reached over and flipped off the receiver.

The deep, dark, abysmally black night had fallen. Low down at the western horizon Earth hung, blue-green and glamorous, just above the crests of many ring mountains. It was a little past first quarter, and it gave only the faintest of light to the tortured and splintered rock formations outside Grimaldi Base. When Earth was full, there would be bright earthlight on the moon, and the moon's surface would look much stranger than any painter of fantastic pictures could imagine.

Inside the base, McCauley was going toward his office when a hand touched his arm. It was Kent. He looked forbidding and grim.

"I'd like to speak to you, sir," he said formidably.

McCauley waved him into the tiny office and closed the door.

"What's it all about?" he asked. He touched a switch and a desk light glowed. He touched another, but nothing in particular seemed to happen. "I've forgotten," he said mildly, "any unpleasant things I may have felt it necessary to say a few hours ago."

"It's Holmes, sir," said Kent, his lips tightly pressed together. "He didn't play fair, sir. When we split that extra air tank he cheated on it. He gave me more than he took himself. And when I was stuck with an avalanche ready to finish me any second, he...."

His voice rose shrilly. He complained bitterly that Holmes had saved his life at least four times.

"He had to," McCauley pointed out. "I said I'd court-martial whichever of you came in, if one came in alone."

"That's the devil of it," said Kent bitterly. "He didn't do it that way! He didn't do it grudgingly. Doggone him, he made me ashamed! If it weren't that I'm hanged if I'll ask any man to overlook things like I've done to him—and he's done to me—if I wouldn't be asking him to overlook so much, I'd...."

McCauley waited. But Kent did not finish. Instead he said savagely:

"As a matter of self-respect, sir, I have to report that Holmes ought to be commended officially for several acts beyond the call of duty, sir—and for a man he hates and who has hated him. That's all, sir!"

He turned to go out.

"Hold it!" McCauley spoke sharply. "You will listen to something. This is an order!" He threw a switch and said: "I recorded your recommendation, Kent. But you will listen to this!"

There was that minute whirring noise a tape recorder makes when it's beginning its run. Kent stiffened. A voice came out of a speaker. But it was not Kent's voice, it was Holmes'. And Kent, staring, heard Holmes saying stiltedly and urgently that Kent had behaved in a highly admirable manner that rated official commendation. He'd risked his life for Holmes on several occasions, and if it weren't that he wouldn't ask any man to forgive him things like he'd done to Kent....

McCauley snapped off the recorder. The sound ceased.

"Holmes came in here first," said McCauley dryly. "His and your recommendations will have due attention. And I'm not going to suggest that you go and shake hands with him, but I think he might like it."

Kent's mouth opened and closed.

"B ... but ..." he stammered.

"Get out of my office!" roared McCauley. "I've got work to do!"

5

(It seemed there wasn't much left to do in the way of space pioneering. There was a Space Platform, and there were bases on the moon, and drone ships had been out to Mars and sunward past Venus. There were new and better fuels, and the problem involving the Van Allen belts of highly charged atomic particles seemed to have been solved. It looked as if the rest of the job of conquering space would be just plain, slogging hard work of a strictly routine nature. This process would be improved a little, and that would be developed a little further, and progress toward the stars would be made by inches. But things never work out simply. There is always something unexpected and usually disastrous turning up. Just when things looked brightest, somebody worked out the causes of solar flares and devised a way to predict them. It looked like a neat and unimportant triumph of pure theory. But when it was closely examined, it meant that the end of all space travel was approaching.)

***

They called Colonel Ed McCauley back from the moon when Doctor Bramwell peevishly refused to go along with the Venus shoot unless the assigned crew was fired and replaced by more respectful men. The top brass felt that McCauley might be able to get along with Bramwell and get the job done. It was a highly necessary job. There was a sun-flare maximum coming up, but if the Bramwell-Faraday screen could be improved enough, it might not matter. Men might continue to occupy the Space Platform, and activities at the bases on the moon might continue. All the men now in space might not have to return to Earth to stay until the flares died down—if they ever did. In effect, if the Bramwell-Faraday screen could be built up to adequate strength, man's conquest of space might continue. If the screen couldn't be built up, space travel must stop.

95

And Doctor Bramwell was the key man in the project. He'd devised the screen in the first place, and was more likely to be able to improve it than anyone else. But he was not an amiable person. So, since he was a civilian and couldn't be given orders, when he said peevishly that he would not go along with the original crew, the men first assigned to the Venus shoot were removed—swearing luridly—and Colonel Ed McCauley came back from the moon to see what he could do.

He had one interview with Bramwell, and was very respectful. Part of the respect was genuine, and part was diplomacy. Bramwell did have one of the two or three best brains on Earth, but his personality gave McCauley reason to be disturbed.

After the interview he consulted higher-ranking officers. He did not think Bramwell was psychologically qualified to take part in the Venus shoot. He thought the scientist would do better work if he stayed home and directed somebody on the ship by tight-beam radio. McCauley spoke forcefully. But Bramwell happened to have a near-monopoly of the kind of brains that were required. And the psychological factor that made McCauley doubtful made the doctor as temperamental as any prima donna. The high brass knew all the reasons for McCauley's protest. But if Bramwell felt himself pushed aside, he'd sulk. If he sulked, he wouldn't do his best work. And his best work was an essential. So McCauley was ordered to make do with Bramwell somehow.

McCauley shrugged dubiously. He asked for Major Randy Hall to be assigned as his second-in-command. Randy gloated when his appointment came through, but McCauley shook his head gloomily.

"There's no reason to feel good about it," he told Randy dourly, in the almost completed Venus ship. "I'll be glad if you go along, but that's not the idea. You're appointed to be the man who'll be fired if Bramwell demands it."

Randy blinked. The cramped, inconvenient, gadget-filled interior of the Venus ship looked glamorous, when you thought of where it was going and what had to be done in it.

"The fact is," said McCauley, "—and the big brass knows it— the fact is that Bramwell's scared. He's terrified at the idea of going out into space. But he's ashamed to admit it. He'd rather die than let anyone know he's in a panic. He's probably trying to keep from admitting it even to himself. So he's making trouble to delay the moment of truth. He's trying to keep from facing the fact that he either has to go or else admit he won't."

"He's afraid of going?" asked Randy incredulously.

"Just as some people are afraid of heights, or spiders, or income-tax forms," said McCauley distastefully. "There's nothing disgraceful about being scared. If he'd only admit it, he could fight it or accept it. In either case he'd be all right. But he insists to himself that he's not only a brainy man but a normally courageous one. So he insists he'll go, and he won't let anybody go in his place, but he can't make himself believe he'll go. So he sets up all sorts of obstacles—crazy ones—ridiculous ones. He doesn't realize it, but he may subconsciously be trying to postpone the shoot until it's too late to make it. If that happens he won't have to face the fact that he's scared."

Randy grimaced.

"And you expect me...."

"To keep him busy," said McCauley. "Try to fix things so that it'll be take-off time before he realizes it. Keep him away from me so he can't pick a quarrel and insist that I be fired. Make yourself the one he'll insist he can't stand, when what he can't stand is the trip."

Randy grimaced again.

"You're a rat," he said resignedly. "But suppose I charm him so he doesn't insist that I be thrown out?"

"Fine!" said McCauley. "There'll be a crew of only two, with him as the third. I'd rather have you than anybody else. But Bramwell's devising excuses for refusing to go. You could be one excuse."

"I'll polish some apples," said Randy, "and fearlessly mixing metaphors, I'll beard him in his den. Maybe I can get so popular he won't want anybody fired."

"Good luck to you," said McCauley skeptically. "You'll need it!"

He plunged into the remaining preparations for the shoot, and Randy went to take over the job of keeping Bramwell from meeting the various people who passionately wanted to have nothing to do with him.

The basic problem the Venus shoot was to attack was at once simple but apparently hopeless. From time to time the sun displays "flares"; these are violent upsurgings of its photosphere, not in the nature of sunspots but somehow associated with them. A flare may begin without obvious warning and in fifteen minutes become monstrously violent, throwing off highly ionized fragments of molecules at the highest speeds material particles can attain. Some of these particles, in time, reach Earth; magnetic storms and auroral displays are the consequences of their arrival. They are harmless to people who live at the bottom of the planet's ocean of air.

But they are not harmless to the crew of a ship in space, or to the staff of that combined way station and observatory which is the Space Platform, or to the occupants of the bases on the moon. The Space Platform itself was set in orbit only three thousand miles out from Earth because of the Van Allen belts of just such particles that have been swung into paths around the earth and form invisible rings more or less resembling the visible rings of Saturn. At three thousand miles out these particles are not deadly. Farther out they are.

It was not until the Bramwell-Faraday screen was devised that it became possible for a man to land upon the moon. With the screen, a man could survive passing through the Van Allen belts in screened ships and set up moon bases. But the margin of safety was not great. It was enough, but barely so.

The Venus shoot was planned because this state of affairs would not last. Astrophysicists had developed a system for predicting solar flares. Then they'd found evidence and, later, proof that the flare frequency was due for an enormous and probably permanent rise. Dense clouds of flare particles would be released. The Van Allen bands would be intensified. Within a year, any man who went beyond Earth's protecting atmosphere could expect to get a fatal dose of radiation burns within an hour's exposure, a flare particle being "radiation" in the same sense as the particles thrown off by radioactive materials. The Bramwell-Faraday screen had to be improved, or else. And the only way to know that it was improved was to try it against stronger and stronger streams of the deadly particles until it failed—or worked. Which meant that somebody had to go out to where flare particles were abundant.

So McCauley labored on the ship that was already nearly set to dive sunward. It would be equipped with the screen that had made Earth-moon travel possible. It would have on board Bramwell, who'd designed the screen to begin with. It would plunge into flare-particle radiation of such intensity that the ship's crew might survive—with the present screen on full—but this was by no means certain. The ship would dive sunward to Venus, swing around that planet, and drift back out to the orbit of Earth. On the way, Bramwell would try to adapt his screen to protect the ship and himself in it. It was a highly melodramatic proceeding, and Bramwell looked very heroic.

But he was a most unpleasant man. Having met him, McCauley estimated his personal attractiveness as much less than one-tenth the personal charm of an irritated skunk.

Ten days after his assignment to the Venus shoot, Randy came to McCauley with a sort of grim humor in his expression.

"I took Bramwell over the ship," he said. "Since he's going to live and work in it, he thought he ought to see it."

"That's reasonable," admitted McCauley.

Randy held up his hand and ticked off on his fingers.

"Item. He drinks a glass of orange juice, a large one, every night before retiring. A supply of orange juice must be provided."

"All right," said McCauley. "Anything else?"

"Item," said Randy. "He is extremely annoyed by noise. He must have a working area that is lined with soundproof material and has a soundproof door so he can have absolute quiet."

McCauley grunted.

"If you can think of anything quieter than space with one's rockets off.... But okay. What else?"

"Item. He suspects he's allergic to the vegetation in the air-freshening system," said Randy. "I promised it would be checked."

"We'll make impressive allergy tests for him," said McCauley. "If that's all...."

"It isn't," said Randy. "He wants a bunk with a hard mattress. He won't use the acceleration chair except for take-off."

McCauley stared.

"But didn't you tell him?..."

"I," said Randy wryly, "am polishing apples. I want to go on this shoot even if he does, which means I want to go very badly. No. I didn't tell him that in free-fall flight with no gravity a steel plate is as comfortable as a down pillow. Why start an argument with a man in a blue funk?... He showed me the reference library he insists he has to take with him. It weighs eight hundred pounds."

"There," said McCauley, "he has to lose! We can't take eight hundred pounds of excess weight. We simply can't do it!"

Randy grinned.

"I showed him a moon-base microfilm reader and offered him the equivalent of four tons of books on half a dozen reels. He couldn't refuse to buy. He only named half a dozen book titles not already on film, and they're being filmed now."

"Anything else?"

"Not so far," said Randy. "He's scared and ashamed of being scared. I don't think he'll actually get up nerve enough to back out, but I'm sure he'll never get the nerve to go. When he finds out the actual take-off time I look for trouble."

"What kind?"

"Maybe hysterics," said Randy. "I'm almost sorry for the guy, but not quite. A man with his brains ought to face the fact that he feels timid, and either fight it or admit it. Especially, a man ought to realize that other people can tell what's the matter with him."

McCauley considered, frowning.

"For your information only," he said, "take-off will be 1400 hours Tuesday, neither plus nor minus. We'll have to stop at the Platform to refuel, and the Platform has a schedule. We'll need to swing very close to Venus for its pull to change our course, and Venus has a schedule. And we'll need to meet Earth farther along in its orbit, and Earth has a schedule. None of them can be changed to humor Bramwell's psychological idiosyncrasies. We take off at 1400 hours Tuesday!"

But Randy shook his head.

"Oh, oh! Friend Ed, we're in trouble!"

"He won't go?"

"He won't go," said Randy. "I'm just learning how to handle him. I believed I could trick him into committing himself so firmly that he'd go, no matter how much something inside of him was screaming that it didn't want to. But Tuesday's too early. I don't think there's a chance to get him either to go or admit he won't. Not by Tuesday."

"That's too bad," said McCauley grimly. "We need him for our crew—him or a reasonable facsimile. Do you know what they used to do when they needed sailors?"

"Pressed them," said Randy. "Press gangs grabbed them. But that was the law then. It isn't now."

"I wasn't thinking of a press gang," said McCauley. "Much more often, a man got shanghaied. We've got to have that souped-up Bramwell screen!"

More days passed. Doctor Bramwell announced firmly that he would not be ready to take off on the Venus shoot on Tuesday at 1400 hours. It was pointed out to him that all the computations for the Venus shoot were based on that time for departure. Doctor Bramwell said firmly that he would not be ready to leave at that time. It was suggested that he name someone who could take his place and work out the improved screen, of course on the basis of his advice and suggestions tight-beamed out to the Venus ship. Doctor Bramwell said indignantly that nobody else was capable of doing his work. But he would not be ready to depart at 1400 hours on Tuesday.

There was a complete impasse. He was immovable. The shoot had to be made at a certain time. He refused to be ready at that time. Preparations for the shoot went on. He calmly and ponderously ignored them.

At 1400 hours on Tuesday a hundred and eighty feet of streamlined, fire-spouting metal plunged skyward from Cape Canaveral. At eighty thousand feet, the first stage dropped off; at seventy miles, the second stage. The third stage, which was the Venus ship, went whipping on out into space. It circled Earth once, gradually overtaking the Space Platform as it floated serenely in emptiness three thousand miles out from the Earth's surface. With tiny, finicky jettings of rocket fuel, and the use of steam-jets for final maneuvering, McCauley brought the Venus ship into contact with the Space Platform.

There was swift and efficient action. Men in space suits swarmed out of the brilliantly sunlit, faceted artificial moon. They connected fuel hoses and topped off the Venus ship's tanks. They floated a second-stage unit out and bolted it in place. They painstakingly got a giant first-stage unit out of the ship lock and set it where it belonged. At the Space Platform, the Venus ship regained the fuel and the ability to accelerate that it had used up getting there.

One and a quarter hours after contact, McCauley reported back to Canaveral that all was well, that Doctor Bramwell was in excellent condition and making no complaints, and that all instruments and equipment had functioned perfectly during the trip from Earth. Then he backed the reenlarged Venus ship away from the Platform.

There was a long, long pause while he adjusted the nose of the ship with micrometric accuracy to an exact, particular spot and made sure that it stayed there. The ship had drifted a good mile from the Platform when he stabbed home the rocket-firing button.

As usual, the instantly following sensation was that of a roof falling in on one and several other roofs falling in on top of it. The Venus ship accelerated for seventy-eight seconds, its nose pointed sunward. McCauley'd set the rocket timer for that length of firing.

When the rockets died, he floated weightless in a ship which had no weight. His head tried to split wide open and let his aching brains run out. His hands were puffy and swollen. His eyes felt as if they were on fire. Beside him, Randy groaned and then growled.

"Doggone the man who invented rockets," said Randy painfully.

"See how Bramwell's doing," grunted McCauley. "I've got to see how we made out."

His headache went slowly away as he checked the ship's line of motion against Earth, growing small behind him, and Venus and the sun ahead. It was reasonably satisfactory. He checked the ship's velocity by the inertia computer and by a tight-beam query back to Earth. His query went back on microwave with a beautifully accurate piezocrystal regulating his frequency. His speed could be determined by the Doppler effect. Both the inertia computer and the Doppler reading indicated that his velocity would need a slight boost later. A time and duration of rocket firing would be computed. So far, though, so good.

"We'd better set up housekeeping," said McCauley. "How's Bramwell?"

"Pulse and respiration okay," reported Randy. "But I bet he busts a button when he wakes up."

McCauley eased out of his acceleration chair. He ached in every bone and muscle from the effects of the two successive take-offs. But he cast an accustomed eye about the ship. It was not a big ship, and Bramwell's stipulated soundproof cabin took up a large part of it. It was, actually, not much more than an oversized moonship. But there were features to be arranged that the short-voyage ships from Earth to moon did not bother with.

McCauley floated over to the packed-up air system. In a space voyage up to a week in length, it is as economical of weight to carry air as to purify it. But the Venus shoot would last much, much longer than a week. So McCauley unpacked the air system. The vegetation had been padded lest it be bruised or broken in the take-offs. He set up the unit and started the hydroponic pump. Randy adjusted the drinkables unit. McCauley set out meals to thaw, in readiness for dinner. Randy put the sanitary facilities and the waste-disposal unit in operation. In effect, the ship had had to be decommissioned as a livable vessel while it was being flung out from Earth as a projectile. Now, in far space and going even farther, the two men transformed it into one of those specialized environments that supply men in emptiness with everything they require except day, night, weight, up, down, normal sounds, and a feeling of belonging where they are.

One homey touch appeared before the recommissioning of the ship was complete. McCauley opened a very small box and took from it an infinitesimal yellow object that stirred as he handled it. It was a tiny canary which had been stowed in the equivalent of a canary-sized acceleration chair. Now it struggled desperately in his hand.

"You'll do, Mr. Perkins," said McCauley. "You're all right!"

He put the panting little creature—Mr. Perkins—into a cage hardly larger than itself. It let out a bewildered chirp when he released it. It struggled wildly, in panic because there was no up or down. McCauley captured it and put its groping claws against the perch. They gripped it. He set up a curiously intricate device inside the cage.

"He'll do," he said in satisfaction. "And it looks as if his food-and-water system is going to work, even in no-gravity. That was a job to design!"

He checked two larger devices with extreme care. One was the flare-particle counter, designed to make an audible click for every hundred, every thousand, or every ten-thousand flare-particle penetrations registered. McCauley set it for hundreds. It clicked every three or four seconds, which was a high concentration but still within the tolerance limit. The other device was the oxygen-supply flutter valve. The plants in the air system would absorb carbon dioxide from the air as the men's breaths produced it, and release oxygen to replace it. But it was not quite a hundred per cent replacement. From time to time more oxygen had to be added from storage tanks to keep the air volume constant and the oxygen percentage right. The flutter valve took care of all this. It made a curiously irritable, buzzing sound when it worked.

The ship went on. Ahead and off to the right lay the steady, last-quarter crescent of Venus. Above and below and on every hand there were stars. Nobody on Earth ever sees the stars as they appear in space. At the bottom of Earth's atmosphere, the keenest eye can see no more than three thousand stars at any one time. Out here one could count as many in a circle no larger than the sun's disk. They shone in innumerable colors. The Milky Way was not a filmy mist across the heavens, but a ribbon of jewels set in pure light; Earth was a glamorous blue-green gem with white spots at its top and bottom, and the moon was a shining smaller circle.

Randy looked outside, as McCauley did. Then Randy yawned,

to hide the awe that every man feels when he looks upon the immensity that men impertinently intend to conquer.

"Well, now," said Randy. "We're well started and maybe a bit of a nap is sensible. Anyhow, Bramwell's sleeping sweetly. Should I loose him?"

"Wait till he wakes," said McCauley. "Things feel pretty good," he added.

Randy was silent, and they savored the feel of the ship together. It was strictly a feeling for technically-minded men. There were innumerable instruments, and all of them registered well within the limits of what it was proper for such instruments to read. The ship was on course, floating in immensity. It had ample reserves of fuel. It had left the Space Platform with all its take-off-from-Earth fuel replaced. Besides, having been launched from the Platform at the proper instant, it had the Platform's orbital speed converted to sunward velocity and reinforced by blasts from the new first-stage booster which was not yet fully expended. The replaced second-stage had not been touched, and there was a third stage in reserve. The air system was functioning. The oxygen flutter valve made a consoling noise toward the ship's stern. It sounded like a staccato Bronx cheer. There was plenty of oxygen stored under tremendous pressure. There were resources of food. And there was all the equipment that Bramwell could possibly need for the development and replacement of the ship's present Bramwell-Faraday screen, so that men could stay in space and go farther and farther from home.

It was while they felt the fine contentment of men with a job to do and the material for doing it that Bramwell awoke. At the beginning he was starkly bewildered. He remembered drinking his glass of orange juice the night before. But he remembered nothing more until he found himself trussed up in an acceleration chair, in no-weight, in space, in the one situation he'd been unable to nerve himself to face.

When he realized what had happened to him, he went into blind, screaming, fighting hysterics.

They were three days on their way when McCauley said patiently:

"I've told you. You can use the communicator back to Earth and protest that you were kidnaped. You can arrange for us to be arrested when we return. But we can't turn back. It isn't possible. I wouldn't if I could. Anyhow you're not nearly as scared as you were. You can think straight, now, certainly! And you can see how ridiculous you'll look if you become known as the man who had to be shanghaied for a space trip because he'd neither the nerve to go nor the intestinal fortitude to admit the fact and let another man try to do his work. If you want to be known as a complete ass, you can. But do you?—Do you want to be known as an utter ass?"

Bramwell glared at him. Nobody can stay panicked for days on end. If a man had had a Damoclean sword hanging over his head for days, he'd wind up accustomed to it. He wouldn't like it, but he couldn't stay scared. Fear is an emergency mechanism to increase the pulse rate and release adrenalin and tone the muscles for combat or flight. It is inherently a limited response. It has a maximum duration.

And Bramwell was now past the limit of the time a man can stay hysterically terrified. He didn't like space. He didn't like no-weight. But most devastatingly and bitterly—now that he was no longer terrified—he was ashamed. McCauley and Randy had seen him in babbling, incoherent frenzy. His dignity was utterly gone. And he hated Randy and McCauley poisonously because they'd seen what he would not admit to himself—that he was afraid. It was humiliation to face them. It was an intolerable rasping-raw of his vanity to be in their presence. They knew he'd been afraid and that he'd bluffed to hide it. They'd seen him crack up when he found himself in space. He was shamed beyond endurance. Therefore he raged, and therefore he hated them irreconcilably.

McCauley went on as patiently as before:

"You can do your work now, and it will never be known that you had to be forced to it like a scared little boy. Or you can not do it, and it won't get done, and the history books will say that men once started for the stars but had to come home because Doctor Bramwell's pride prevented him from working on the problem he was the only man who could solve."

Randy, watching, nodded to himself. McCauley was doing a

good job of argument. That last "only man who could" was flattery, and Bramwell ought to respond to it.

"I shall charge," said Bramwell spitefully, "that you two prevented me from doing my work by imposing impossible working conditions on me!"

"Name possible ones," said McCauley patiently, "and you'll get them if they're available."

The canary, Mr. Perkins, chirped from its cage. The bird was upside down in relation to Bramwell, but it seemed to have adjusted admirably to the conditions of space travel.

"The soundproofed room," said Bramwell triumphantly, "is ridiculously small. I need more space. But above all I need quiet! I need to be isolated from the society of fools and from noises I cannot endure!"

Mr. Perkins chirped again. The canary was still bewildered, but at least it could see now, and it'd found out how to get at its food and water, and it felt quite cheerful.

"... And you might start," rasped Bramwell, "by strangling that blasted canary! I abominate canaries!"

"Things are looking up, Ed," Randy said cheerfully. "There can't be anything very much wrong with a man who hates dogs, children, and canary birds!"

But McCauley had begun thoughtfully to examine the layout of the interior of the ship.

They were two weeks on the way toward Venus. The flare-particle counter clicked every second and a half. The sun's disk, ahead, was appreciably larger and Venus was a thinner crescent than before. Earth was a small object, though still larger than Venus, and the moon was very small indeed. At this distance the Space Platform was, of course, invisible. But the changes inside the ship were more marked than those outside.

The interior of the ship was now divided into two parts. McCauley and Randy had pulled down the small cubicle made of soundproofing material that had been built for Bramwell to work in. They had used the same material to wall off a full half of the ship. There was a door in the wall, and part of the air-freshening system operated through sound baffles so that the air in the walled-off space was changed, quite silently, with the same regularity as the air in the forward end of the ship, where McCauley and Randy did their work.

But McCauley was vaguely disturbed. It had developed gradually, but he did not feel right. Even though he could not become physically exhausted in a total absence of gravity, he felt dull and weary. There were measurements of flare-particle frequency to be recorded, both from outside the ship where the Bramwell-Faraday screen did not operate, and from inside where it did. The figures were curiously difficult to copy. But there was no reason for him to feel weak and stupid. The air system worked perfectly. The food was adequate. The ship moved steadily, silently, perfectly on its way at a certain number of miles per second, which was increasing a trifle because of the sun's gravitational field. Everything seemed perfect. But he didn't feel right. Randy was not himself, either. And Mr. Perkins sang only half-heartedly.

The canary began, now, what started out to be a beautifully executed trill, but which died away after half a dozen tremolos.

"Mr. Perkins isn't in good voice today. What's troubling him?" Randy spoke with a certain effort.

McCauley concentrated on the report he was filling out. He shook his head and looked again; he was startled.

"Look here!" he said sharply. "We had the screen on when we left the Platform. It kept out the radiation when we went through the Van Allen belt. But now we're nearer the sun. Stuff's coming through the screen! It's been coming through for days! And we haven't noticed it! What's the matter with us?"

"I wouldn't know," said Randy listlessly.

"We're not on the ball," said McCauley. "We've got to do something about this!"

He rose from his chair. It took but the slightest of effort, and he floated free. He reached out his hand to the wall and directed the motion of his whole body. He approached the soundproof barrier that now divided the ship into two separate parts. He caught a handhold on the door and knocked.

Minutes later the door opened. There was no gravity, so Bramwell did not stand in the opening. He floated there, scowling.

He and McCauley faced each other, very much like swimmers, except that they swam in air.

"Radiation's coming through the screen," said McCauley. "It shouldn't. Not this early, anyhow. Shouldn't something be done? I'm ordered to consult you about all adjustments of the screen."

He was vaguely dissatisfied with himself for asking. He should not have to ask anyone for instructions. He was ordered to in this case, but decisions were his job.

"Turn it up!" said Bramwell peevishly. Then he seemed to notice that he had not been actively unpleasant. He moved quickly to correct the omission. "How many times," he demanded furiously, "have I told you not to disturb me! Noise upsets me! Leave me alone! Isn't it enough that I have to share the ship with clods, without having you bang on my door?" He glared around the forward part of the ship. Mr. Perkins sang again, a half-hearted attempt at a warble. "Noise! Noise! Noise!" rasped Bramwell.

He pulled the door shut. McCauley floated lethargically to the screen unit and made an adjustment.

Nothing important apparently happened, but something ceased to happen so often. The sharp, slightly irregular clicking of the particle counter seemed to stop. It was a full five seconds before it clicked again, six before it clicked a second time, and five before it clicked a third.

"I wish," said McCauley lethargically, "that I'd been a little more on the job. Why didn't we notice the radiation count going up, Randy?"

"Bramwell complains if we touch the side of the ship because it makes noises inside his sanctum," Randy answered. "Maybe we've been trying not to think for fear the noise would disturb him."

McCauley considered the comment carefully, which was itself an indication that he was not up to par.

"No," he said slowly, "it's not that. But we don't feel right. Maybe we'd better take our temperatures. It would be ghastly if we were getting sick! Bramwell couldn't feed himself, let alone get the ship around Venus!"

With some effort he found a clinical thermometer. But they did not have any fever. In fact, their temperatures were considerably lower than the 98.6° F. which is considered the norm for men in good health.

They were two weeks and five days on their way. McCauley shook his head to clear his mind. He reread what he had just written in the ship's log, vaguely puzzled because it did not seem to make sense. With enormous effort he checked each word and found that he had left one out here and another one there. With great determination he put them in. Somewhere in his mind there was a feeling that he needed to do something very urgently, but he could not think what it was.

"Randy," he said, and something in his brain noted that his voice was plaintive, "I can't seem to think straight! There's something I ought to do! What is it?"

Randy shook his head. He floated in the straps of his acceleration chair; not that the chair was needed, but because it held him still so that there was no possible chance of his striking against the unmuffled wall of the ship and so sending a solid-conduction sound back to Bramwell.

"I don't know," said Randy flatly. "I don't feel too bright myself."

The soundproof door of the after compartment opened. Bramwell came out. Somehow he looked pathetic and frustrated, but he essayed rage.

"I have to have silence!" he cried ferociously. "You are making noises! I cannot think! And I must think! I have to have silence!"

McCauley said numbly:

"I'm sitting here, and Randy's in his chair. There's no noise."

"There is noise, or why can't I think? You are doing something to keep me from thinking!... That canary! It has been singing! That's it! You must wring its neck so I can think!"

"No," said McCauley, "it hasn't been singing. It hasn't sung for a long time. It did, but it doesn't any more. Why?"

"Something is the matter!" insisted Bramwell desperately. "I'm stupid! I'm as stupid as you! And I must use my brains!"

"You've got everything we can give you," said McCauley without particular emphasis. "We can't seem to do our work right either."

110

"There is some new condition we do not know about," Bramwell said, in a sort of puny panic. "There is something in space which is working to destroy us! Here! Send this message back to Earth!" McCauley took the slip of paper on which words were written in an erratic, spidery hand. "But I think you are making noises!"

Bramwell pulled himself back into his soundproof half of the ship. The door closed behind him, but not quite in time to cut off the beginning of an agitated whimpering sound.

McCauley pushed the beam-on button. He should have checked the time, Earth time, to see if Canaveral were on the side of Earth from which it could pick up the beamed message from space. It wasn't, but he didn't think to check. He read, in a monotone, the message Bramwell had written out:

I feel the purpose impossible probable effect similar to X-rays with this is vital to further but I have no instruments.
                                                                    Bramwell.

He was vaguely puzzled but he read it faithfully. Then, without checking for reception, he turned off the transmitter. He went back to the painful task of trying to make the ship's log entry at which he'd been working for a long time. He assured himself that though the message did not mean anything to him, they'd understand it back on Earth.

But they didn't. It didn't get back to Earth. The Venus ship had been pointed very accurately so that the parabolic reflector for the tight beam to Earth was perfectly aligned. But Bramwell had protested the faint, faint hum of the gyros which kept the ship pointed correctly. McCauley had turned them off. He'd meant to re-align the ship for each period of communication, but his mind was confused and he forgot.

Earth had received no message from the Venus ship for six days past. There was consternation in the Space Service.

It wouldn't have lessened any had Bramwell's message been picked up. He'd meant to say that he felt that achievement of the Venus ship's purpose was impossible because of something which doomed the men in it. He thought it probable that some previously unnoticed effect of radiation, perhaps similar to X-rays, was destroying their capacity to think. This effect should be studied. It was vital to further space exploration. But he had no instruments that could detect it.

They were three weeks out from Earth. The Bramwell-Faraday screen was turned up to full strength, and still the radiation counter clicked and clicked. It now indicated a higher frequency of radiation-particle penetration than was experienced in any of the Van Allen bands around Earth. Bramwell was a pitiable figure. Enough of his mental capacity remained to inform him of his intellectual degeneration. Now and again he popped into the forward part of the ship, trying to catch McCauley or Randy at some activity that was stealing his brain power away. When he failed to do so, he reacted with rages that would have been alarming except that he had not the energy for anything more than words.

McCauley struggled against a massive indifference. One part of his mind stood aside and knew that the occupants of the ship were doomed, but he could not care. Mr. Perkins no longer moved about its cage. Its feathers fluffed, the bird might be dead on its perch. McCauley tried painstakingly to write up the ship's log, but what he wrote was confused, meaningless. Even his handwriting grew steadily more illegible.

Then, at three weeks and one day, the leak alarms rang stridently. They made a frightful clamor all over the ship. The few compartment doors closed tightly.

"Leak," muttered McCauley to himself. "Prob'ly meteorite. Got to get in suit and fix leak...."

Fighting an overwhelming lethargy, he floated toward the space suit rack, missed it by yards, doggedly made his way back to it, and numbly began to get into a suit. Randy worked at the same task. He stopped to rest.

"Randy," said McCauley protestingly. "Get in suit! Leak!"

He himself was incredibly feeble. Had there been weight in the ship, he could not have lifted his helmet to his head. He settled it over his shoulders, but his fingers failed to turn the thumbnuts tight. Even so, there was the familiar feel of air blowing across his face.

Strength came to him. Not instantly, but with the first breaths of air from the suit tank his head seemed to clear a little. After more breaths, his hands moved assuredly. He began to realize the change in himself and gulped down deep lungfuls of the dry, curiously flat-smelling stored air.

Randy hadn't finished getting into his suit; he seemed to have gone to sleep. But when McCauley approached him in the space suit, Randy's eyes turned toward him incuriously.

McCauley thrust him into the space suit and clamped down the helmet. Randy suddenly stared.

"Something's been wrong with the ship's air!" snapped McCauley, feeling more like himself every second. "It's no good! Breathe deep, Randy! Breathe deep!"

Randy obeyed. His eyes cleared.

"Bramwell!" snapped McCauley. "Get him in a suit! He hasn't sense enough to do it himself!"

He flung himself at the control board. The leak was....

But there was no leak. The leak alarm had rung, but every pressure indicator in every part of the ship showed the same figure. It was.... McCauley gazed incredulously at the dials. The ship's interior pressure was 12.8 pounds to the square inch as against a normal 14.7. The difference was enough to set off the leak alarm, but a thinning of the air like this was not enough to cause the stupidity, the lethargy, the confused and helpless thinking which McCauley—marveling—realized had appeared during the past three weeks.

He heard a howling noise between the clamors of the gongs. It was Bramwell.

"You're making a noise!" wailed Bramwell. "I can't have a noise! I must have quiet...."

McCauley spoke crisply into the transmitter, sending a tight-beam message back to Earth. It would be minutes before it was received, as against the less-than-two-second lag in a message sent from the moon to Earth.

"We were suffering from oxygen starvation," said McCauley

briskly. "The plants in the air-system's hydroponic garden absorbed carbon dioxide and gave off oxygen, but not quite cent per cent. There was a steady small loss of oxygen in the ship, caused by the use of oxygen as well as carbon by the growing plants. This small loss should have been made up by the addition of oxygen to keep the volume of the ship's air constant. But it happened that the oxygen flutter valve became jammed...."

He heard an explosive sigh of relief behind him, but he carefully did not look up at Bramwell. Bramwell was very silent these days, and he practiced extreme self-control. He realized now that he'd let too many things bother him. But he was still bothered, and horribly so, by the memory of his inability to make up his mind to face the journey in space, or to arrange for somebody to substitute for him, so he'd had to be shanghaied. He was even more bothered by the memory of his behavior when he found himself in a ship off for a swing in to Venus and out again. McCauley and Randy ignored these past happenings, and Bramwell would never be able to bring himself to mention them. But he was very much ashamed.

The thing that disturbed him most, however—the thing that made him extremely conscientious and extremely self-controlled—was the consequences of not facing things and of trying to cover up his own shortcomings. When he got over his hysterics he wanted to get even with McCauley and Randy by defying them. But he hadn't dared defy them openly. He'd been peevish and ashamed and humiliated. To him the bronx cheer of the oxygen flutter valve had seemed a mockery. But he still felt superior to pieces of machinery. So when the flutter valve went "Tht-tht-tht-tht!" at him, he angrily turned it off. And the human race almost had to stay on Earth forever because of it. The three of them came very close to dying.

McCauley continued talking matter-of-factly into the transmitter.

"As a result of the jammed valve, there was a steady lowering of the oxygen content of the air, but the carbon dioxide content did not increase. The air was getting closer and closer to pure nitrogen all the time, but we didn't notice, because a person feels suffocated by an excess of carbon dioxide rather than by a lack of oxygen. We were all dying quite comfortably when the leak alarm went off because the air pressure was dropping as the oxygen left us. When the alarm went off, we found the trouble and brought the oxygen concentration up to what it should be. We think there should be no more trouble. In fact...."

He stood up and handed the microphone to Bramwell. Bramwell hesitated a moment. Then he spoke.

"I have to report that the problem of a stronger Bramwell-Faraday screen field seems to be solved. This particular accident suggested a theory. Quite coincidentally, the theory resembled one aspect of charged-particle theory. It led to an idea. The new screen has a very gratifying reflex action which uses the velocity of the flare particles themselves to increase the screen's resistance. The charged particles are tricked into defeating themselves. I will have a detailed account of the theory and the apparatus shortly."

Mr. Perkins, in its cage against the wall, burst into song. The canary began with a trill and went on to a warble; then Mr. Perkins essayed a glocken. He accomplished it triumphantly. Bramwell scowled at it from habit. But then he carefully smoothed out his forehead as he handed the microphone back to McCauley. He nodded at the tiny cage.

"Not bad," he admitted. "Not bad at all!"

The Venus ship got back to its rendezvous with Earth some four months and eighteen days after take-off. At that time, this was the longest space journey ever made by man. But it was not only the longest trip. As a result of it, the reflex Bramwell screen had been developed along a new principle: The higher the velocity of a charged particle, the firmer the screen's resistance to its passage. Since the screen could stop even the highest-energy cosmic particles, the effect of such particles upon living matter could be determined by comparing exposed organisms—human beings and all other living things on Earth—to other organisms shielded from cosmic radiation. The ship, too, had made some close-range infrared photographs of Venus and prepared a fairly complete map of the planetary features underneath the cloud bank. The length of Venus' day was established. The....

It was a highly successful expedition from all standpoints.

But Randy insisted that the most remarkable result was the change in Bramwell. There was no doubt that Bramwell had one of the best brains in the solar system. Even when they disliked him most, both McCauley and Randy had respected his brains. But after Bramwell found out that they'd never refer to the way he acted before and immediately after he was shanghaied, the fact that he was so ashamed of himself improved him as far as human society was concerned.

He improved so much, in fact, that by the time they got back to Earth, McCauley and Randy were not much more polite to him than they were to each other.

Which was high honor.

(As a brand-new lieutenant, McCauley had been the first man to ride a rocket out of atmosphere. As a major, he was in the first piloted space craft to achieve an orbit and land again in one piece, and he helped to build the Space Platform. But it seemed likely that after he made colonel he was likely to be stuck with administrative tasks and go on no more trips. There was the affair of the Bramwell-Faraday screen, to be sure, but that was pure luck. He gloomily expected nothing more exciting than desk duty in some deadly tedious minor base upon the moon. But it happened that the asteroid Eros—very small, very irregular in shape, and very, very eccentric in its orbit—was due to pass close to Earth again as it went out from the sun. It had passed within two million miles of Earth in the 1930s, and nothing happened. But now McCauley was looking for an excuse to be more than a desk Colonel. He added up Eros and Mars and drone rockets, and the resources of the Space Service and a certain amount of imagination. He came up with something the Space Service had believed was still twenty years in the future. He'd worked out a way to get back from Mars. So he was assigned to try it.)

****

The Personnel Ship of the First Martian Expedition was within two million miles of Mars when McCauley missed his watch. Everything had gone along as predicted, up to that moment. The ship had taken off from Earth and headed outward for its rendezvous with the tiny asteroid Eros. It burned rocket fuel lavishly to get the necessary velocity for the journey. Then it floated interminably while Earth grew small and far away behind it, and the sun dwindled and its heat lessened. Then Eros appeared like the tiniest pinpoint of light, and the ship drew up to it and braked—it had very little fuel left for its braking—and touched, and then moored itself to the half acre of previously moored bales and cases and special drones that the asteroid had ferried out from Earth. The ship's crew went outside in space suits, each one separately tethered to the ship by a long cable. They began to check the condition of their waiting supplies. Everything had to be examined because it had lain—hung—rested for two years on Eros' surface in the network of cables and drill rods needed to hold it there. The condition of the stores was satisfactory. So Colonel Ed McCauley took a shower.

In its way, even that was an adventure. The ship, of course, had no gravitational field, and Eros was very small indeed. Of almost solid nickel-iron, it was five miles by two by three; and though it dwarfed the ship, its gravity pull was on the order of one five-millionth that of Earth. So taking a shower in a ship moored to Eros was something special. It meant holding fast to handholds in a furious fan-made gale that blew water against one and then blew it off and to a water collector where it could be filtered and sterilized and pumped around to the showerhead again. It was quite different from a bath on Earth, but McCauley was much refreshed. He toweled himself and put on his ship clothes again—and his watch was gone from the pocket he'd put it in.

It made no sense at all.

He was still looking for the watch in every corner of the compartment outside the shower tank, when Major Randy Hall came in, propelling himself in that extremely unlikely fashion which has to be used in zero gravity.

"Randy," said McCauley vexedly, "I've lost my watch."

"I lost mine a week ago," said Randy. He caught a handhold and pulled himself to a sitting position, resting on nothing whatever. "Hathaway lost his the week we started out. Fallon told me privately that somebody'd swiped his wallet only a day or so after we started out."

McCauley swung around to face him.

"That's nonsense!" he said angrily. "It's lunacy! Who'd want to steal in a space ship?"

"I thought it was lunacy, too," said Randy, "until a few minutes ago. Now I'm more credulous. From checking supplies outside, it appears that some very fancy small instruments are missing. A case was broken open. Since we tied up here."

McCauley stared at him. On the face of it, Randy's statement was flatly impossible. Personal character aside, it was unthinkable that a member of the Expedition should steal from another member or from its stores. Nobody could use a stolen article in a ship containing exactly five other men. Nobody could sell stolen goods to his fellow crewmen. And nobody could hope to take any loot back to Earth. If all went well, the men themselves might hope to get back to Earth at some problematic future time. But every ounce of Earth-bound cargo would be scientific material, mostly microfilm. Stolen goods couldn't be used or sold or taken back to Earth. Money itself wasn't worth stealing. Nothing was. Many millions of dollars' worth of equipment now outside the ship had lain unguarded and untouched for two years in empty space. Nobody had stolen any of it before. There was no sense in stealing it now.

But somebody was.

It was a serious matter because of its implications rather than the facts themselves. The First Martian Expedition needed everything its members could give it for the safety of them all. If somebody considered himself apart from the rest, if one member of the crew was willing to injure the others by stealing from them, the situation was very, very bad. In fact, having a thief among the six was like a serious accident occurring to the Expedition's equipment. It would be comparable to a vital defect in the miniature atom-pile which was to supply energy for them to live by when they reached Mars' surface.

In a sense, though, the Expedition itself was the result of an accident of a different sort. The first part of this coincidence was the fact that some two years earlier the asteroid Eros had passed close to Earth on its elongated elliptical orbit around the sun. Eros is one of those rock and metal fragments which are found most often in orbits between Mars and Jupiter. Some people maintain that they are fragments of a planet which exploded some hundreds of millions of years ago, and there is some evidence to back this view. For one thing, some circle the sun in extremely eccentric paths. Eros swings out at its farthest between Mars and Jupiter, but when nearest the sun it dives in between Earth and Venus. Sometimes— rarely—it comes close to Earth in its passage across Earth's orbit. This had happened two years ago.

The second part of the coincidence was the purely fortuitous fact that only two Earth-years later Eros would pass even closer to the planet Mars. The two accidents added up to an opportunity, when McCauley added rockets and other resources of the Space Service. And the Service seized it.

So two years ago Colonel Ed McCauley had landed a ship on the asteroid, then close to Earth. He'd led a work crew which drove drill holes into the asteroid's solid metal substance. They made anchorages to fasten supplies to, and McCauley'd anchored the supplies. Then he took his ship back to Earth. On the way he'd passed other ships going out to Eros. They also anchored supplies on it. In one hectic month, the Space Service unloaded on the tiny asteroid all the supplies and equipment—some two hundred-odd tons of it—that the First Martian Expedition would need not only on Mars, but in getting back from Mars, which was equally important. Then the Space Service waited.

Nearly two years later, but now some months ago, the ship that was now moored to Eros took off from Earth. Enormous amounts of fuel were required for the journey out to Mars. No ship could carry fuel for the trip and the landing, much less a return trip. But if a ship made a rendezvous with Eros when the asteroid was close to Mars, it could refuel from the stores waiting on Eros. It could guide drone rockets from Eros to landings on Mars, carrying more supplies. The drones would not even need to be ships. They could be mere outlines of ships, with motors and guidance systems, their cargo lashed to their framework. So the asteroid would serve as a cargo carrier for the supplies the Expedition required, and also as the landing craft needed to put them ashore on the red planet.

So far, everything had worked out. Very shortly the first of the drones would be sent off to land the first cargo near an oasis close to the summer pole of Mars. Others would follow till all had been sent out; then the ship, refueled, would leave Eros and overtake the equipment that had preceded it. Its crew would recover the landed rocket cargoes, set up a base, be well equipped and amply supplied for several months of Martian exploration, and then have adequate fuel for the voyage home. More than that, it would leave a base that was ready to function, and fuel for return flights, for a reasonable number of other ships in the future. In fact, the passage of Eros close to Earth and then to Mars had provided a freight service that meant the difference between men going to Mars and staying home.

But there was a thief among the six men making the first trip. There was McCauley and Randy Hall and Fallon and Brett and Soames. Hathaway was the meteorologist who would learn all that was to be known about Mars' atmosphere. Fallon was the atom-power mechanic. Brett and Soames had their specialties, but all had been trained in the remote control of drone rockets with their loads of precious material. All were needed.

"Hmmm," said McCauley, frowning. "You say Hathaway and Fallon lost things, the one a watch and the other a wallet. You and I ... I lost an electric watch. It runs on a battery the size of a pea. I never have to wind it." He looked up. "Are you sure Brett and Soames haven't lost anything?"

Randy looked curiously at McCauley.

"Come to think of it, Brett asked me if I'd seen his fancy gold pen. That was weeks ago. He uses an issue pen now. And I think—I think Soames was turning things upside down once, looking for some sort of gold luck-piece he carries. Yes. He did."

"I'll find the stuff," said McCauley, frowning, "but I'm bothered."

He looked out a port at the crew members on the surface of the asteroid. Randy followed his eyes. The four other members of the Expedition, in bulky space suits, worked busily in a landscape—or an Eros-scape—too fantastic to be real. All of them now accepted the view that Eros was an explosion-created fragment of something much larger, and that that something must have been remarkable. Nine-tenths of the surface of Eros was solid metal such as forms the core of all the heavier planets. Now, metal rods stuck here and there out of drill holes in the raw, glistening crystalline mass. Between the drill rods ran cables holding nets under which objects were tethered. There were drone rockets by the dozen, and bales and boxes and tanks seemingly by the hundred. They would drift away to nowhere but for the nets which held them fast. They'd been held thus during two years of unaccompanied, uneventful cartage from the orbit of Earth out to the orbit of Mars. Most of the stuff needed only to be sorted and loaded on the drones, which would take off under control by the drone-master keyboard on the ship. There was an enormous mass of supplies. There could be a loss of up to fifty per cent in transit without irreparable damage being done to the Expedition's purposes.

When Randy looked back from the laboring, space-suited figures outside, he was alone. McCauley had gone to the ship's small workshop, all of whose tools would be left in the base on Mars. Frowning, he connected a microphone and an audio amplifier and a headset and went back to explain to Randy. But Randy was no longer there. He'd gone outside to carry on as second-in-command. His business was largely finding things to worry about and telling McCauley, who made them turn out all right.

McCauley went purposefully through the ship with his microphone-amplifier unit, touching it here and there against the fabric of the vessel. The idea was perfectly simple. If there was a thief on board, he would certainly not keep his loot on his person or in his locker. He'd have a hiding place for it. The loot included McCauley's watch, which would not run down for months. And solid things conduct sound much better than air does. The ticking of a watch which can't be heard at five feet, in air, can be heard through fifty feet of wood or metal if the watch is in contact with the farther end.

So McCauley methodically listened for the ticking of a watch conducted through the metal of a spaceship. There was no one else on board. There was no operating machinery to make extraneous noises. Presently he heard the five-times-a-second click-click of his watch. He traced it to its loudest, unscrewed a floorplate, and found three watches, a very expensive gold pencil, and a luck-piece that was a gold coin some hundreds of years old. There were also three small and very expensive instruments that came from a smashed case on the asteroid.

McCauley put them in his pocket and went to the compartment that was his sanctum as commander of the ship. He pulled out the personnel report on one member of the crew. It was not believable.... Then he thought of something. He pushed the outside-communicator button.

"Fallon," he said, "report to the ship. A job for you."

He drummed on the desk before him as he waited for Fallon. This was a singularly unpleasant situation.

Fallon came in, still in his space suit. He opened the faceplate and grinned. He was an exuberant personality, this Fallon.

"Reporting in, Colonel."

Without a word, McCauley brought out the three watches, the instruments, the elaborate gold pencil, and the luck-piece. He picked out his own watch and the instruments and waved his hand toward the rest.

"Get these back where they belong," he ordered. "I'll take care of the instruments. Don't let anybody know they're being returned. Let it appear they've been found misplaced."

Fallon stared. Then he went white and licked his lips. But he said nothing.

"I found this stuff," said McCauley, "as soon as I looked for it. I knew you'd hidden it, because you said your wallet was gone and there was no wallet with the other missing stuff. You should have put it in with the rest of the loot, Fallon, if you wanted to be convincing."

Fallon stared.

"It's about as stupid a performance as I've ever heard of," said McCauley. "Why did you do it?"

Fallon swallowed. Then he braced himself and looked defiant. In a moment or two he managed a grin. It was a shaky grin, but he straightened up and then shrugged.

"Why should I tell you?" he said. "What can you do about it, anyway?"

"I can think of a few things," said McCauley.

"Name one!" said Fallon defiantly. "You can't kill me. You can't put me out of the ship, because that'd kill me. You can't lock me up, because you need everybody. You can't do anything! You might as well forget it! This trip was dull. I wanted some excitement. I thought there'd be a big fuss when things started to disappear. There wasn't. All right, I'll put the stuff back. But you might as well forget the whole business because you can't do a thing about it."

McCauley stiffened. Fallon was right. There wasn't anything he could do, in the ordinary sense of the word. He couldn't execute Fallon for theft. He couldn't imprison him. If he punished him in any way that aroused his resentment, Fallon could no longer be trusted, and any of the six men could destroy the other five simply by neglecting some essential duty assigned to him. In space, men have to trust each other and be worthy of trust in return. There is no room in unlimited emptiness for a man who arouses suspicion and antagonism among his shipmates solely for his own amusement. But Fallon had done just that. He was as dangerous as an atom bomb on the expedition to Mars. But whereas an atom bomb can be disarmed, nobody can disarm a man who chooses to play the fool.

Fallon picked up the objects McCauley had given him. He spoke with sudden truculence.

"Well?" he said. "What can you do? Just suppose I don't feel like giving these things back. I'm going to, but if I wouldn't do it, what'd you do?... You won't even tell the rest you caught me! You want the stuff put back without their knowing it was taken!"

"Yes-s-s," McCauley said very slowly. "That's right. I shan't tell the rest. I want things to go along smoothly, without squabbles or suspicions. But you want excitement, more than our job provides. You'll look for it in some other fashion now, won't you?"

Fallon said defiantly:

"I'll do what I feel like doing!"

"Yes," said McCauley, nodding. "You'll get your excitement regardless. You're as independent as a hog on ice, because you think that I can't do anything to stop you. Very well. I'll try to provide you with some excitement. You do what you please. I'll do what I please about it."

Fallon's eyes narrowed.

"You don't care what I do?" he demanded skeptically.

"I do care," McCauley told him. "You're the one who doesn't

care. But I'll be able to make use of you somehow. All right; you can go, now."

Fallon hesitated, scowling. Then he went out. He was uneasy. He could have understood had McCauley threatened him, or flown into a rage, or possibly tried to appeal to a nonexistent loyalty to his companions or to the purposes of the Expedition. But McCauley had not reacted in any fashion that Fallon could understand.

Later in the day Randy consulted with McCauley.

"Funny thing happened," he said vexedly. "Fallon went around and gave Brett back his fancy gold pen. He said he'd taken it for a joke. He gave Soames back his luck-piece and Hathaway his watch. He explained that they were jokes, too. He gave me mine.... Did you get yours back?"

McCauley nodded. He explained what had happened. Randy blinked.

"But why didn't he just slip them back like you told him to?"

"He's worried," said McCauley. "I didn't threaten and I didn't reason with him. So he figures that I've something special in mind. So he wants to be on good terms with everybody but me. Now if I accused him of stealing, he could insist that he was joking and that he'd proved it."

"That's crazy!" said Randy.

McCauley did not contradict him. He shrugged. Presently Randy went out on the surface of Eros. A single incautious movement might send him floating off into emptiness except for the moorings to the drilled-in metal rods that anchored supplies and ship and crew alike. On the nickel-iron surface of the asteroid, to be sure, magnetic-soled shoes ought to hold a man down. But the emergency wasn't great enough to make depending on them necessary. Everyone kept himself anchored to a drill rod, and did not let go, anywhere, until another anchorage had been secured.

The five-mile-long and two-mile-thick mass that was Eros floated onward in its orbit. It rotated very slowly—its day was half an hour and its night was thirty minutes—and all the stars appeared in turn, including that nearest star which was the sun. The Milky Way spread incredibly across the sky. Earth was blue-green and a bare speck of a crescent—a crescent because it was to sunward, and a speck because it was well over forty millions of miles away. Mars, to the outward, was a perceptible disk the size of a quarter at forty feet. Already photographs taken on spaceships and sent back to Earth by scanning signal had disclosed features that even the giant telescopes on the moon had not detected. Randy claimed to have seen Phobos and Deimos with his naked eye, and perhaps he had. But most of the crew were too busy for more than an occasional glance out at Mars.

The supply items to be carried by each drone rocket had to be regrouped so that no one rocket would contain a disproportionate amount of any one kind of supplies. It was to be expected that some loads would be lost, so it was important to make sure that no one load, if it was not landed or recovered, would cause crippling shortages of this item or that.

There was, though, one bit of freight that would not be trusted to rocket transport. The fuel for the atom-pile would go on the ship, because if the ship did not land safely there'd be no Expedition, and if it landed safely, the atomic fuel would be essential. The thin air of Mars would have to be pumped up to the pressure required by the human body, and its oxygen would have to be concentrated. There would be need for heat during the bitter Martian nights. Power was necessary for human life on Mars. And only atomic power would be adequate.

The first drone rocket lifted off Eros when the asteroid was a million and a half miles from Mars. The rocket rushed ahead, dwindling until it could no longer be seen among the stars. It carried a tank of rocket fuel, a rocket motor, and a communications unit. That was all. The drone was not streamlined, not pretty. It was a skeleton with its drive at the tail, a shaft to tie the cargo to, and a television camera at its nose. The first loads shipped were relatively unimportant ones, so that initial disasters due to lack of experience would have the least serious consequences. When the asteroid was a quarter of a million miles farther on, more rockets were on the way. There were two near-disasters. The rockets were prepared for launching during the planetoid's half-hour "daylight," but they were launched when the launching site was away from the sun and toward Mars farther out. During daylight McCauley prepared one rocket for firing and returned to the ship. Later Hathaway went out to set off that "night's" salvo. The first rocket blew itself to bits when fired. Hathaway had a very narrow escape.

The men figured out, afterward, that in the utter cold of the planetoid's "night" the rocket motor had cooled to the brittle point of metal. When the rocket was fired, the frozen metal flew apart before it could warm up and thus restore normal strength throughout its thickness. McCauley berated himself to Randy, because he had not anticipated this fact. The rest of the salvo was held until "sunset" the next day, and was fired within five minutes of the coming of darkness, before the metal could cool to brittleness.

The other near-tragedy happened when a rocket took off and the flame splashed against a glistening metallic upcrop and licked fiercely at Soames' space-suited legs. He jumped convulsively, rose out of the flame before it could either cook his legs or melt down his space suit, and, gasping in horror, soared off and up to the length of his safety rope. The rocket went past him no more than a dozen feet away. Its exhaust could have burned him to a crisp, or at the least flashed his plastic faceplate. That was a very close call indeed.

Presently Fallon came looking for McCauley. The mechanic was coming off-shift and still wore his space suit. He opened the faceplate, grinning nervously.

"Look here, Colonel," he said ingratiatingly, "I've got something I want to say to you."

"Go ahead," said McCauley. He was still bitterly discontented with himself. Actually, Soames should not have been so near the rocket blast, but McCauley felt responsible because he hadn't ordered him specifically away.

"Soames had a pretty close call," said Fallon nervously.

"Yes," said McCauley curtly.

"Hathaway had another," said Fallon. "When that rocket blew, he could have been killed. He should've been."

"I know it," snapped McCauley.

"I ... I ..." Fallon hesitated. "Look, Colonel! We had a— disagreement. I acted like a fool. I want to apologize."

McCauley scowled. There were innumerable things to worry about, and Fallon was one of them. McCauley had taken the one line that might keep Fallon from making trouble. He'd scared him, and it seemed to have worked. But for Fallon to come to apologize was something else. It meant that his attitude had changed from almost mutinous defiance to panic.

"Forget it," said McCauley.

"I—didn't have you figured right," said Fallon shakily. "I thought you were ... just the usual kind of character. I ... I know better now. I'd—I'd like to ... well ... you're likely to need somebody to help you. Maybe you don't think so, but if you knew you could count on me...."

Fallon's voice practically clicked off, and McCauley realized that he was terrified. The man was afraid to say something, but he was more afraid not to.

"What would I need you for besides your duty?"

Fallon hesitated, licked his lips, and then said desperately:

"Soames and Hathaway—they almost got theirs. I've been thinking. If ... accidents happened to us ... to all but you...."

"Go on," said McCauley, frowning.

"We're ... sending most of the stuff to Mars," stammered Fallon. "B-but we're keeping the atom fuel on the ship. It's w-worth a lot. If something happened to most of us ... why ... two men could take the ship back to Earth and land it anywhere they wanted to. And if ... if a person had contacts, that atom fuel would be w-worth a lot. Millions."

McCauley was jolted.

"Suppose," he said grimly, "that you tell me the rest of your idea."

"Why ... why ..." Fallon tried hard to be ingratiating and confidential, but he couldn't make it. So he said harshly: "I'm going to tell you something. My name's Fallon, but I'm not the Fallon you think I am. I've got a brother. He was slated to come on this trip. I was in the pen. I broke out. They were close after me. I went to my brother for money and help. He's tried to help me before, tried to make me stay out of trouble. This time was the worst, but this time he wouldn't help me any more. It was too serious. So I ... slugged him and took his papers and his orders and reported for duty instead of him. I ... I guess he couldn't bring himself to turn me in, but he figured I'd be caught before take-off. But I bluffed it through!" Here a trace of pride came into his voice. "I bluffed it through, and I came on the trip in his place because there wouldn't be anybody hunting me out here."

McCauley did not display any feeling at all. That Fallon had committed a crime or crimes back on Earth—forty million miles away—meant nothing here. Not if he did his work. But....

"Well?" said McCauley.

"I'm telling you," said Fallon urgently. "You didn't tell the others that I'd lifted their stuff. You had to have a reason. Then Hathaway almost got it when that rocket blew. And Soames came close to frying in a rocket blast. There are too many queer things happening! You not telling the others on me, and then...."

McCauley sat perfectly still, staring at Fallon.

"It adds up," said Fallon defiantly. "There's millions in atom fuel here. If things happen to the others, you can get back to Earth and land anywhere, and if you've got contacts so you can sell the atom stuff...."

McCauley waited ominously. Fallon tried to go on, and could not. But his meaning was clear. In some twisted fashion he had worked out what he believed a logical explanation for McCauley's behavior to him. It implied that McCauley did not see the Mars expedition as a normal man would see it, but as an opportunity for the first space robbery in history and perhaps the most stupendous criminal coup since time began. It was true that the atomic fuel for the Mars reactor had a money value in the tens of millions. To McCauley, that fact would mean that it was something to be guarded and taken care of. But to Fallon, it was something to be stolen. And he thought McCauley saw it the same way.

"I suppose," said McCauley evenly, "that you've guessed that I plan to kill off the others and go back to Earth alone. Is that it?"

Fallon twitched nervously.

"It figures," he said desperately. "But you need another man to help! I told you who I am. I couldn't afford to double-cross you! I couldn't land this ship. But I could help a lot!"

"Yes," agreed McCauley with irony, "you could. So you want to throw in with me, eh?"

"Y-yes."

"All right," said McCauley. "You're in. You share in everything I do and everything I get out of it. It's a bargain."

"F-fine," said Fallon in a voice like a croak.

He'd try to believe it, but he wouldn't be able to be sure. He left. McCauley knew that he would quake and be terrified, and he would not believe in McCauley's intention to make him a partner in crime. But in his own view he couldn't do anything but try to bargain for his own life if—but he thought of it as when—McCauley murdered or abandoned the others in emptiness.

McCauley told Randy the whole business, of course. As second-in-command Randy needed to know everything.

"He's a swine," Randy said distastefully. "But it took nerve to try to bluff through our training period, with the voyage out here to follow it."

"He's in bad shape," said McCauley. "However he got started that way, he chose to be a crook at some time or another. He probably thought it was smart. It wasn't, but now he can't think the way a non-crook thinks."

Randy frowned, thinking.

"I believe," Randy said slowly, "that I'll explain to the others. He's with us and the way he thinks has to be allowed for. They won't let him know they're on to him.... I feel sorry for the poor devil. You will, too, when you think it over. They'll feel the same way."

McCauley nodded. Space is no place for the self-righteous or the intolerant. Charity is a requisite for the endurance of journey in emptiness, in closed tin cans with re-breathed air and enforced exasperating contact with other persons. The Mars Expedition members had been chosen for personality traits as well as technical competence. It was remarkable that Fallon had been able to imitate his brother's character well enough to avoid unmasking before take-off.

The work of the Expedition went on. In the half-hour day, the rockets for Mars were loaded and set up for firing. Immediately after darkness fell, they went streaking away from the small, misshapen asteroid. McCauley or Randy at the control board picked up their monitor signals one by one, verified their course and speed, and made such adjustments as would be needed to get them to the planet which men now ought to reach a good twenty years ahead of schedule. Near Mars, they'd be swung into orbit and landed one by one.

It became routine. But it was a hair-raising routine. There was a tissue-thin difference between the success and failure that meant life or death. What rest they took was in snatches. But things went along. Curiously enough, when Hathaway and Brett and Soames were told in confidence of Fallon's self-produced predicament, it amounted to easing the tension their continuous labor might have produced. They had something to think about besides the nerve-racking need for absolute accuracy and absolute care in all they did out of the ship. Crawling about under the cargo nets was harrowing. There were the stars. There was the feeling of absolute emptiness, into which their sensations assured them that they were falling unendingly.

But Fallon had no relief as the others did. He didn't have their purpose. They were risking their lives to accomplish something they wanted to do. That was why they were here. But Fallon was with them in flight from the law. He had only fear to sustain him.

Three-fourths of the rockets had been released. Nine-tenths. There were more than forty rockets aground on Mars and the ship was refueled, and already it would be possible to leave Eros and land on Mars and set up the base and do the work the Expedition was expected to do. They could do all this and then return to Earth. The rockets still in space and on Eros amounted to a margin beyond necessity, and every extra one that landed would increase the surplus of equipment and supplies.

And then Fallon got lost. He was never out of sight of the others, but he got lost. It was the rule, of course, for every man to have his own life line securely fastened to solidity. They were long life lines to permit movement about the cargo cache and the much-diminished heaps of stores. They were inconvenient, but they were starkly necessary. It was strictly forbidden for any man at any time not to be safely tethered. And....

A rocket was to be made ready for firing. Its cargo was brought to it, item by item. Fallon had worked with the others. He was treated with singular forbearance by his shipmates. There came a moment when somebody had to shift his space-rope anchorage. It happened to be Fallon who needed to do this. Soames took hold of Fallon's space rope in the middle and held it firmly while Fallon shifted the end to another anchorage. Fallon was nervous, worried. He finished the task quickly and went on toward the cargo items he was to move.

McCauley, prowling on his perpetual task of inspection, saw the knot Fallon had made. He said sharply:

"Fallon, stop moving and hold on to something solid."

Fallon swung about and stared apprehensively. He clung to an anchor rod sunk in the metal of the asteroid. McCauley made sure he was safe, untied the space-rope knot, and tied it more securely.

"It was a bad knot," said McCauley. "You're safe now."

McCauley went on. This was outside the cargo-netted space and near where the rockets went up. Fallon clung fast to the drill rod. The others went about their business. Stars blazed in the daylight sky. The sun flamed far, far away. Fallon stayed motionless, gripping the rod that was securely set into the metal of Eros.

Presently he stirred stealthily and tugged at the rope with the new knot in the end. It was firm. He tugged more strongly. It held. Then, with the gentlest and most fearful of tuggings, he drew himself to where McCauley had fastened his space rope. He examined McCauley's knot. Fallon was afraid of McCauley, because he had made a bargain he did not believe McCauley would keep. He believed that McCauley meant to be the sole survivor of the Mars Expedition, returning secretly to Earth with tens of millions in stolen atomic fuel.

And Fallon believed that McCauley had planned the near-tragedies of Hathaway and Soames. Therefore he believed that McCauley would be arranging more successful accidents for those two and the rest, and that because Fallon knew of McCauley's plans, he, Fallon, would be the first to be destroyed.

He could see nothing the matter with the knot, but he distrusted it with a despairing terror.

He untied it so he could retie it himself. And McCauley's voice roared in the headphones in his helmet:

"Fallon! What are you doing?"

Fallon started violently. He jumped. His space rope was not anchored, and Eros has no measurable gravity. Fallon went up and away from the asteroid, toward a thousand million light-years of emptiness. His space rope rose with him, not trailing behind but writhing and twisting weightlessly, more like a tendril of smoke than anything else. Horror filled him. He could not cry out.

"Get him!" roared McCauley.

Space-suited figures turned in the stark white sunlight, and inky black shadows followed their movements in strict synchrony. Fallon was twenty feet high.... Forty. A space-suited figure jerked at his space rope for assurance and then leaped up toward Fallon. It was a miss. The glittering metallic space suit swung in a wide arc and then down to ground again. A second man leaped. A third. They swept past the line of his flight. The space rope of one of the men touched Fallon's. Had it struck near the middle, it might have brought his rope down captive. But the end of Fallon's rope flicked free and he went on toward the stars.

Now there were babblings. Space-armored figures moved swiftly toward a single spot, pulling themselves by their ropes.... Fallon was sixty feet high.... Seventy.

Then a man came soaring straight upward. He missed Fallon, but he flailed a rope and it tangled in Fallon's. The bobbing, rope-held figure hauled in, and had Fallon's rope fast. He wrapped it swiftly about his arm. When the jerk came it was not severe.

Then a single figure on the asteroid pulled down and down and down, and Fallon was towed to solidity. He touched before he could utter a sound.

McCauley was the man who'd hauled him back. The others crouched or squatted down, holding fast to the metallic projections from the surface of Eros. They'd given up their ropes to make a rope long enough for his rescue. While one went after him and McCauley stood erect to draw him back, the others held fast by their fingertips to keep from sharing his predicament. They'd risked floating away as helplessly as he himself, in order that their life lines might be used to save him.

McCauley did not reprimand Fallon, but he pointedly thanked the others for the promptness with which they'd acted.

Later, Randy asked vexedly:

"What was the matter with Fallon? He knew he shouldn't have unfastened his rope!"

"His knot wasn't good, and I retied it," said McCauley dryly. "But he thinks I intend to kill everybody, probably him first. So when I meddled with his life rope he thought I was arranging his death. He meant to retie the knot to defeat my evil intention."

"He's a fool!" snapped Randy. "We'd better have it out with him, or there's no telling what he'll do next!"

"I'm afraid I have to," McCauley said distastefully. "He'll be humiliated when he finds out I was humoring him. But get him, anyhow."

There was a clanking sound somewhere in the ship. The inner air-lock door closed. There were noises that told of the sealing dogs being tightened. Then, immediately, the outside lock door opened. Randy went to find Fallon. He came back, disturbed.

"Fallon just went outside. He's supposed to be off-duty, too."

McCauley frowned. Then he flipped the outside-communicator switch. As a matter-of-fact precaution, there was two-way communication with emptiness whenever anybody was outside the ship. Anything that came in was immediately heard from speakers all over the ship, so that the control room did not have to be manned all the time work was proceeding on the planetoid's surface. If an emergency arose, everybody anywhere in the ship would know immediately.

"Fallon," said McCauley curtly into the outside transmitter, "you're wanted. Come back, please."

Silence. No answer. There was only darkness outside the ship now. Stars moved steadily up from the blackness that was one nearby horizon, and down to the blackness that was the other. The red disk of Mars—very near, now—was the brightest object in the heavens.

"Fallon!" snapped McCauley. "You're wanted! Return to the ship immediately!"

A clanking sound came from all the loud-speakers inside the ship. Then Fallon's voice.

"Wait a minute." He panted as if doing some heavy labor where there was no weight. "Ah-h-h! Right! What do you want?"

"I want you back in the ship," said McCauley sternly.

More clankings. They were the type of sound that might be heard inside an air-filled space suit and picked up by its helmet microphone.

"What are you doing?" demanded McCauley.

"I'm fixing ... uh!..." The last was a grunt. "I'm fixing a way to settle something.... I'm set now."

"Fallon!" barked McCauley. "Come to the ship immediately! That's an order!"

"I'm busy," said Fallon's voice, defiantly. "But I'll tell you something! I'm not going back to Earth with the rest of you. I was on the run when I passed myself off as somebody else and got on the ship. I was on the run from Death Row in the pen. They had me ready for the hot seat in two days more, and I got away. Why should I go back to Earth?"

He paused. And then he said, his tone indescribable:

"Everybody is hearing me. I fixed that! I doctored the aerial switch so when it's turned on it can't be turned off again! McCauley can't keep you from hearing me now, because he called me! And McCauley's going to squirm now! I joined up with him to wipe out every one of you, so we could go back to Earth with the atom fuel to sell to contacts he's got! He tried to kill Soames and he tried to kill Hathaway! He tried to kill me today, by getting me lost, but the rest of you jumped to help me and he had to join in so you wouldn't know what he'd tried!"

McCauley winced.

"Poor fool!" Randy said.

"Now listen," said Fallon's voice fiercely. "I've told you the truth. If I'd told you before you wouldn't've believed me. But you're going to believe me now, because I've scrapped my chance of living—it wasn't good anyhow—to tell you! You watch McCauley!

Send word back to Earth of what I've told you. He'll not dare to do a thing when a dying man's accused him—and that's what I am!"

"Fallon!" barked McCauley again. "It's a mistake! You thought I planned that stuff, and I was just playing along with you! The others knew all about it! They knew everything you just told them! It's a lie! I'm not planning anything. I just played along with you...."

"Yes?" jeered Fallon. "Tell that to the aviators! The spacemen don't believe you!" Then he said: "So what? I'll be the first man on Mars! I'm Joe Fallon, 4272365, Walla Walla Penitentiary, and I'll go down in the history books. I'm taking off for Mars. Want to race?"

There was a sudden roaring. It was the sound of a rocket blast, conducted by metal to a space suit and picked up by the microphone inside.

"T-taking off," gasped Fallon, outside. "You get this story back to Earth and he won't dare do anything! He won't dare! But I didn't rat on him! Only on what he was going to do."

After that, there was only the roar of the rocket blast.

They poured out of the ship in space suits as fast as the air lock would let them. Perhaps some of them had a faint, faint hope that it was merely a joke. But it wasn't. There were boxes and bales floating heavily, soggily, in the emptiness about Eros. They had been thrust aside when Fallon took the rocket for himself. And he was gone.

McCauley made an irresolute movement back toward the ship, and Randy said quickly, via space phone:

"No use, Ed! We can't make more than six gees acceleration in the ship, and in a loadless rocket he'll make twelve! We can't catch him!"

And there'd be nothing they could do if they did catch him. McCauley ground his teeth, staring at the star-filled sky.

"I did something wrong," he said bitterly. "Something wrong! But what would have been the right thing?"

Hathaway said enviously:

"He'll be the first man on Mars, at that! But his air won't last all the way. He'll coast in and crash and never know it. But he'll be the first man on Mars!"

"Yes," said Randy wryly, "he'll have that.... Let's get these last rockets off and land at a respectful distance behind him."

And they did.

Of course, as everyone knows, the First Martian Expedition was a great success. Of the six men who left on it, five came back. They had maps and photographs and petrological samples, and a complete and surprisingly reasonable explanation of the canals and oases about which astronomers had argued for the best part of a century. They even brought back a sluggish, naked, squirming creature which initiated an entirely new line of biological research.

McCauley began a battle behind closed doors, and Randy helped him, and in time a curious error in the public records appeared. It is officially stated in all the books that one Joe Fallon was the first man to land on Mars, though the first records of the Expedition gave his name as Andrew—at least Fallon the crewman was not named Joe. There is a strange lethargy in official quarters. Nobody bothers to correct the records.

"Of course," said McCauley to Randy, "he stole our watches, but he was a pretty decent character at that, considering. He'd have no part in taking your lives."

"What was he sentenced for?" asked Randy suddenly.

"First-degree murder," said McCauley shortly. "I was curious too. I asked." Then he said, "They're talking about trying to make Jupiter, Randy. It seems to me that if we try, we can get to go on that job. What do you say?"

Randy grinned. He put out his hand and they shook on it.

(When Ed McCauley was a very young officer—in fact a new-made first lieutenant, space travel was only for robots. Nobody'd ever ridden out of the atmosphere in a rocket, and nobody'd ever piloted a ship into orbital flight and landed it again; there wasn't a Space Platform, and the moon bases hadn't been built. There was constant danger from cosmic rays and flare particles, and nobody dreamed of trying to reach either Venus or Mars.

By the time McCauley was a colonel, all those things had been done. But oddly enough, it didn't seem that the job was finished. The more that was done, the more remained to be done. And McCauley found that things never got any more settled down.

There was Venus to be explored, right next door, and Mercury just beyond that. And Titan looked promising, and of course there were the asteroids, of which one or two urgently required examination. And even when there were settlements on Saturn and Uranus and Neptune, there were rumors of a planet beyond Pluto.... And after that, the stars.

There'd never be any end to the journeyings of men into space.)

THE END